RELEASE!

A Walker Brothers Novel

J.S. SCOTT

Release!

Proofread by Alicia Carmical – AVC Proofreading
Cover Design by Cali MacKay – Covers by Cali

ISBN: 978-1-939962-62-1 (E-Book)
ISBN: 978-1-939962-63-8 (Paperback)

CONTENTS

PROLOGUE

Trace

SIX YEARS AGO...

*P*lease. God! Just let him live.

I was so wired up on coffee that I couldn't think straight. Staring down at my youngest brother, Dane, in a hospital bed, I kept hoping I was in the middle of a nightmare.

If I'm dreaming, I need to wake the fuck up!

Clenching my fists on the side rail of his bed, I wanted to openly cry. But I wouldn't. I couldn't.

My father was dead.

Karen was dead.

All I had left were Sebastian and Dane, the latter barely clinging to life, and I wasn't letting go of my baby brother. I'd already lost too much, and my sanity couldn't take another death.

Had it not been for the fact that Sebastian and I had finals, we would have been on that private jet when it had crashed, but we'd left Vegas three days earlier. I'd only had time to attend the nuptials, and had headed straight back to college for my finals. So had my middle brother, Sebastian. Newly graduated from high school, Dane had lingered, hanging out with a friend who lived in Sin City for a few days before heading back to Texas with my father and his new wife, Karen.

Grief tried to consume me as I thought about my dad, but I wouldn't let it. Right now, I *needed* control. At the ripe old age of twenty-one, I was a new college grad, ready to move on to finish my MBA.

Unexpectedly, I was also now the head of the Walker family, thrust into a position I didn't think I was ready to take. But as the oldest, what choice did I have? Everybody was coming to me for decisions now, and I needed to pull my shit together.

I prayed to a God whose existence I'd highly doubted in the past, willing to try *anything* to keep Dane alive.

The doctors said even if he makes it, Dane will be scarred. Like I give a shit about that? I just want him fucking breathing on his own, free of the ventilator that now mechanically pushed in Dane's every breath.

I could barely see his eyes, but on closer inspection, I could tell that they were still closed.

Dammit!

I started breathing shallow, my heart racing a mile a minute. What if he *doesn't* make it? What if I lose him, too?

The protective gear I was wearing to keep the room free of germs and lessen Dane's risk of infection to his burns was stifling me.

Shit!

Get Control! Get Control!

I need to bury my emotions, push them deep inside me. I have people depending on me right now, including Dane. I refused to lose hope. The doctors hadn't exactly given me good news, but my youngest brother was a fighter. He'd make it through.

I'd been trained since grade school to take my father's place when the time came. I just hadn't known it would be so damn soon. Vaguely, I knew I was going to have to step into his shoes, and finish my MBA while I was taking his place.

I balked at the thought of my father being dead. I hadn't quite dealt with it yet.

Suddenly, I heard a voice in my head, my father's voice:

Son, if you fall apart and lose control, everything and everybody around you will, too.

He was right.

In the past, we'd always had Dad to lean on, and he was the strongest man I'd ever known. If he had weaknesses, I'd never seen them. Maybe I thought he'd never die, that he wielded too much power to ever have the life sucked away from him. The thought made me feel suddenly vulnerable, but there was no time for me to be a pussy. Now, I had to go it alone, let everybody lean on me. It didn't matter if I was ready or not.

My eyes caught a blur of motion outside the hospital door, and I saw Sebastian gearing up to come in.

He's here.

I'd known he was on his way, but I was surprised at how fast he'd gotten here. My brother's expression was grim as he donned a pair of gloves. A pretty nurse stepped forward to help him secure his mask.

Sebastian still had college to finish, and Dane hadn't even started. I was going to be the one they'd look to for support. Although Sebastian was only a little over a year younger than me, he'd never gotten the same guidance my father had given me because he was younger and had different goals.

Both of my brothers need me.

Something suddenly *snapped* inside me as my eyes met Sebastian's through the glass of the hospital room door. He looked as shell-shocked, exhausted, and hopeless as I felt right now.

Don't show it! I can't let him know I'm overwhelmed and having problems dealing with everything that's happening right now. He needs me, and Dane's going to need me just as much.

I forced myself to nod at Sebastian, trying to silently signal to him that everything would be okay, but I could tell he wasn't quite buying it.

We both knew that our lives had been profoundly changed in a matter of moments, and that nothing would ever be the same again.

CHAPTER ONE

Eva

THE PRESENT...

"*M*r. Walker is ready for you now." The disapproving female voice was attached to a body and face that could easily belong to a supermodel.

I looked at the woman, tilting my chin just a little as I stood. I was poor, I was hungry, and I was desperate. But I'd be damned if I'd let *Ms. Perfect* know that. Maybe it was obvious that I wasn't rich, but I'd never let her know that I was intimidated by my lack of funds. I wasn't as impressed by billionaires as my mother had been, and I'd never longed for wealth.

All I'd ever really wanted was to live a happy life, an existence without fear. So far, I hadn't gotten there...yet. But I refused to give up trying.

People are people, and the rich can be just as evil as a person stuck in poverty.

I nodded at her. "Thank you." Not that I was grateful that she'd kept me waiting for hours just to talk to her boss, but I said the words because I was used to being polite. My father had taught me good manners from the time I was able to speak. He'd always said that you get what you give. I'd found his theory a bit flawed over the years since he'd died, but I did believe he was, for the most part, correct. So I did try to remember his words, and I tried to be cordial to everyone.

Unfortunately, my Latina side wasn't always as patient as my dad had been.

I'd been waiting nearly all day in the downtown Denver sky-scraper that belonged entirely to Walker Enterprises just to see *him*. Trace Walker was a man I was inclined to dislike, but he was my only hope at the moment, and I was a survivor.

Trying to act like I belonged on the top floor of this elegant building—which I didn't—I strode across the office until I reached the perfectly put together blonde female, trying my best to look dignified in a pair of torn blue jeans and a t-shirt that had seen better days. My dark, curly hair was neatly pulled into a tie at the back of my neck. Still, I knew I probably looked exactly like what I was: a poor woman who didn't have a cent to her name.

Some of the *nicer* people would call me a latte, or a spicy cracker. Half Mexican and half Caucasian, I was actually what the *not-so-nice* people called a mongrel or a mutt. Just like a mixed breed dog, I didn't know where I fit into the world, or exactly who I was. All I knew was that I'd stooped low enough to seek out a Walker, which meant that I had nowhere else to turn now.

Ms. Perfect opened the door to Trace Walker's inner sanctum like it was a solemn occasion. I wondered if she ever smiled, and if she did, what would happen? Mostly likely, her face would crack. Her tight, stoic, frowning expression hadn't broken all damn day, even though I'd been unfailingly pleasant to her.

Obviously, she didn't much care what she gave...or what she got back. Not when it came to a woman like me anyway.

I brushed by her, trying *not* to get another glimpse of her snooty expression. For hours, she'd been looking at me like I was a cockroach that needed squashing, and I was getting tired of it. There was a limit to my affability.

When I had finally entered Trace Walker's office, I didn't notice the classy contemporary décor or the expensive modern art on the wall. I didn't see the amazing floor to ceiling windows that exposed an incredible view of the city from the top floor. It wasn't because his office didn't encompass all of those things and more. I just...

I couldn't.

My eyes riveted immediately on *him*, and I was incapable of looking away.

Trying to remind myself that I *couldn't* and *wouldn't* actually *like* him, I walked slowly toward his enormous desk, unable to ignore the wholly masculine pheromones that seemed to emanate from his massive form.

I'd heard stories that he was formidable, controlled. Unconcerned, I'd blown off the information. How scary could a twenty-seven-year-old guy be, even if he *was* filthy rich?

Now, I was thinking the stories I'd heard about him were probably true. People were drawn to him for some reason, his presence magnetic. And he hadn't even spoken a word.

I sat in the luxurious chair in front of his desk, taking him in, trying to size him up as I heard the quiet click of his secretary closing the door. He was all money, and all class...everything I *wasn't*. His long, masculine fingers flew across the keyboard on the desk as he stared at the computer screen, looking displeased.

Even irritated, Trace Walker was probably the handsomest man I'd ever seen.

His hair was short, thick, coarse, and a mixture of various shades of brown. The stubble on his face nearly hid what looked like a strong jaw and classically sculpted features. Studying him from my seated position, I couldn't quite make out the color of his eyes, but he had eyelashes some women would probably kill for.

The fact that he was dressed in a power suit that I was certain was custom made was also rather daunting. It made him less approachable to a woman dressed in rags.

J.S. Scott

What was I thinking to finagle my way into the penthouse in the Walker building, wanting to speak to Trace Walker himself?

He was breathtaking, powerful, and obviously very much in control of this particular domain, no matter how young he might be. I wanted to jump out of the chair and run back to my apartment with my tail between my legs.

I could always resort to my 'plan B' which was to travel a little with my few belongings, go somewhere to start over...or would I be starting to live for the first time? But who was I fooling? I could never outrun my past.

When I'd decided to take on this bold mission, 'plan A', I definitely hadn't been prepared for *him*.

His commanding voice stopped me from taking any action. "What do you want?"

The husky baritone startled me, so it took me a moment to speak. "I need a job." I had a difficult time not stuttering, but I managed. I wasn't the type of woman to be intimidated by someone with money, but it wasn't the fact that Trace Walker was filthy rich that flustered me. It was *him*. The air in the room almost visibly sparked with his energy, his presence, the commanding, controlled tone of his voice.

Jesus, he was intimidating for a man who was only four years older than I was, but then, we shared very few commonalities except for one.

"Ah, you're the friend Chloe sent?" He turned in his chair slowly.

Finally, he was looking at me, and the dark green eyes that were suddenly trained on me freaked me out. His stare was intense, assessing, and I had a feeling that his quick examination, which seemed to bore into my soul, had found me somehow...lacking.

"Chloe?" I had no idea who the woman he mentioned was, but he was obviously recognizing me for someone I...wasn't.

"Chloe is my cousin's wife. Didn't you know that?"

I shook my head. I didn't know who Chloe was, much less who she had married.

He continued. "She told me she had a friend in Denver who might be able to use a temporary job, a woman who might work for the position I require. I assume you're that woman."

My pulse started to race. *A job*, much needed work that I *desperately* wanted to acquire. I knew it was wrong, but I answered, "What kind of work?" My voice was shaky, and I hated it. Cowardice had never been a trait I possessed, and it wouldn't get me the work I so desperately needed. But this situation was out of my scope of life experience.

"She didn't explain?" His eyebrows rose as he continued to stare.

"No." I kept my answers simple. It was easier that way.

He looked me up and down, examining everything from my hair to the holes in my beat-up sneakers. It made me feel like a sample beneath a microscope, but I willed myself not to squirm under his less-than-admiring gaze.

"You're not what I expected," he mused, folding his arms in front of him on the desk. "But I'm short on time. The holidays are coming, and I need this situation resolved."

He was abrupt, businesslike, and I felt like a waste of his time. Apparently, he needed help, but resented spending any time on acquiring it.

"I can gift wrap," I told him in a rush. "I can cook, and I have experience in cleaning and housekeeping." He obviously needed someone to help him for the holidays. Even if it was a temporary job, I needed the work. "I can even be your personal shopper. Tell me what you need and I'll find it."

A slight smile started to form on his face. "Chloe really didn't fill you in at all, did she? Unfortunately, she didn't tell me much about you, either. She just said she had a friend who might be able to help me. What in the hell is your name?"

My full name was a mouthful: Evangelina Guadalupe Morales. I settled for answering, "Eva."

"I don't need a maid, or a personal shopper." His smile faded and his eyes were suddenly alive with fire, with an intensity that was slightly alarming. "I need a fiancée."

Okay. For the first time in my life, I was pretty much speechless. It took me a while to stop gaping at him and recover enough to speak. I could only mutter one word. "Why?"

"My reasons are personal, and the position is temporary. I need to be engaged for the holidays. After that, I'll no longer need your services." He eyed me critically. "You have to be convincing. One of the first priorities will be a wardrobe and makeover if you decide you can accept the job without demanding anything except what I'm willing to pay. You take orders directly from me and you follow them. Nobody else knows the truth. Understand?"

Oh, I understood perfectly. Somebody had hurt him, and he wanted that person to believe he didn't care about them anymore, that he had moved on. I could tell this wasn't about a business deal to him. He needed to appear engaged because it was personal to him. I shouldn't do this. I couldn't do this. But the offer of money to simply play a part for a short time was so incredibly tempting. "What's the pay?" I blurted out the question before I could stop myself. A hungry woman was a desperate one.

"Fifty thousand. Twenty-five up front, and the other half when the job is completed." His voice was businesslike and abrupt.

I swallowed hard to get rid of the lump in throat. "Fifty thousand dollars?" My voice came out squeaky, and it was probably because of the severe shock I was experiencing. A woman like me didn't see that much money at one time in her entire lifetime. Who in their right mind paid that much money just to even the score with an ex-lover? "I can't take that kind of money." Regretfully, I *had* to decline. I wasn't Chloe's friend, and sooner or later he'd figure that out. Besides, I couldn't take advantage of someone who had been hurt so badly, even if he *was* a Walker. I might be hungry, but my damn conscience was going to let me starve.

"How much?" His answer was clipped and slightly angry.

Our eyes met as he barked out the question, leaving me feeling raw, exposed, and just like the imposter I was. "I just wanted a job," I answered breathlessly. "I want something permanent. I was hoping maybe I could get a position in one of your resorts. I'd work hard, and I have some experience in housekeeping."

It wasn't a lie. I did have experience in housekeeping, until I'd lost the job shortly after I'd started.

All I wanted was to escape my past life, work a job that could provide a steady income, and not be afraid anymore.

Trace looked at me like he didn't understand me at all. His eyebrows drew together and I could see the muscle in his jaw grow tight.

Finally, he asked huskily, "You just want a cleaning job?"

I nodded slowly. I wanted *a* job. Any job that would be permanent. Trace Walker owned the largest resort company in the world. Walker Escapes was known for being plush, offering a luxury experience without the over-the-top price. I'd gotten let go from my last position a month ago. I couldn't pay my rent, and I was just one short step away from being homeless...again. A job—any kind of work I was capable of doing—was what I was desperately seeking. I'd approached Trace Walker for a reason, but it wasn't because I wanted to be his temporary fiancée.

He contemplated me carefully before answering. "I could send you anywhere in the world. I have resorts everywhere."

"I know. I don't care. I just need work, Mr. Walker. Please." The pleading in my voice bothered me, but I was beyond pride and in survival mode. My future depended on how this meeting turned out.

"No family?" His eyes watched for any reaction.

"None." I was being truthful. If I had any family, I wouldn't be *here.*

The longer he stayed silent, the more nervous I became. My breathing started to get fast and shallow, and my chest ached from my heart racing so fast I was afraid it was going to stop from the exertion.

Trace leaned back in his chair and ran a hand through his hair. "I can get you a job. As long as you're a good employee, you'll have security at one of my resorts. If you help me, I'll help you. Half the money up front, and then I place you wherever I have an opening after the assignment is over."

I'd have security? It was something I'd never experienced. Every job—every single moment really—I was worried. Even when I had a position, I'd been desperately afraid I was going to lose it if anyone found out about my past. Security? I didn't know the meaning of the word.

I was tempted, so very tempted. I could have money in the bank, not be afraid of overdrawing my checking account. I would be able to eat, to breathe. However, I knew I couldn't take the deal. "I'm not Chloe's friend," I admitted quietly, sadly.

My hopes had risen and then plummeted. I couldn't lie to him. I did want that elusive protection of having a stable job, but it wouldn't be possible if he didn't know the truth.

A small grin split his face. "I know. I'm glad you admitted that yourself. At least I know you're honest."

I gaped at him in surprise. "How did you know?"

Trace shrugged. "Chloe *did* tell me that her friend was an executive assistant who could possibly help me over the holidays. I don't think she needs a permanent job. She just wanted the extra cash." He paused before adding, "I have to admit that you have a lot of guts approaching me directly. Had I known you were looking for other employment, you would have been sent to human resources. I was under the impression that you were Chloe's friend."

Chloe, whoever she was, probably didn't hang out with women like me. "I don't look like somebody who would be her friend, I'm sure."

"No, you don't. She'd never see a friend in desperate need and not help her. Chloe is a former Colter."

I looked at him in surprise. "The Colorado Colter family? Senator Colter's family?" I wasn't much into keeping up with current affairs, but there probably wasn't a single person in Colorado who didn't know about the wealthy Colter clan. "I definitely wouldn't be friends with a billionaire," I muttered quietly. I might live in the same state as the Colter family, but I was an entire world apart from people like them.

"Are you going to take my offer?" Trace's voice was back to being businesslike.

I paused for a moment. Even though I desperately needed the money, I really should tell him everything, but the thought of that elusive *security* stopped me. Longing overtook my common sense. What did it matter now? I'd gotten what I'd come for. If the time came when I had to tell him everything, at least I'd done a job that I'd get paid for doing. And I made a silent promise not to let him down. "I'll do what you want if I have your promise that you'll send me to a fulltime job afterwards. I might need help with choosing a little better clothing if I'm going to be convincing as your love interest." I had no idea what rich people were currently wearing.

I desperately wanted to laugh at the thought of meaning *anything* to this magnetic, impossibly attractive, and incredibly wealthy man.

A mixed race street rat with a history like mine?

Not happening!

"You're going to need more than just clothes," he observed critically. "And you'll take all the money I offered *and* the job. You'll need it to get started in a new position."

His bossy tone sent shivers up my spine. Unfortunately, he was right. I was going to have to find a new place to live and bear the travel costs. "Half up front, and the job." I'd compromise.

"All of it," he demanded stubbornly, almost angrily.

Looking at him was dangerous, but I met his commanding glare with equal determination—for all the good it did me. He wasn't going to bend. The stubborn tick of the muscle of his jaw told me he wasn't budging.

I didn't want to argue and risk the chance of losing my opportunity.

I sighed. "Okay." If I agreed, I could always take what I really needed and return the rest later if the job panned out. "Is this really that important to you?"

He nodded abruptly, sending a stray lock of hair to fall onto his forehead. "Very."

"Can you at least tell me why?"

"You hungry?" Trace ignored the question.

My stomach rumbled as if on cue. "I'm starving." I decided that being honest about most things would make the situation smoother with this man. He might be incredibly hot, but he was all business. He also seemed to appreciate honesty.

"I'll take you to get something to eat. We can talk." He efficiently shut down his computer and stood.

Air left my lungs in a rush as I surveyed his height, his strength, and the broad, masculine form that filled out his custom suit so very well.

What was I thinking? I could never pull off being a fiancée to a man like *him.*

"I don't think that's a good idea." I stood up, but my feet felt rooted to the ground.

"We both need to eat. I want food," he insisted. "How long has it been since you ate?"

"Four days, five hours and about ten minutes," I answered automatically because I was currently feeling every moment of the food deprivation.

"Are you serious?" His question came out growly and displeased.

"Completely."

"Let's go," he answered brusquely, walking around the desk to take my upper arm lightly. "Damn, you're thin, and you look like you're barely out of high school. How old are you?"

I snorted. "I'm twenty-three, hardly high-school age."

"You look like jailbait," Trace answered gruffly.

"I can show you my identification." I knew I looked young with my hair pulled back and no makeup on my face. Haircuts and makeup were a luxury I couldn't afford.

"Not necessary. I believe you. But we're changing your look." He propelled me gently toward the door.

I shrugged. I didn't care what I had to do to play the part. I just wanted the promised job. "Fine."

I let him lead me out the door, noting with relief that *Ms. Perfect* was gone, probably done for the day.

"You're going to eat," he answered bossily.

My first reaction was to rebel because he was ordering me around, but I squelched it. He was my boss now, so I needed to do what he wanted for a while. As my stomach growled, I knew I'd really have no problem with that particular command.

CHAPTER TWO

Eva

"This place is a dive," Trace grumbled as he dug into a massive pile of Mexican food that was overflowing a decorative paper plate.

I stopped shoveling food into my face long enough to look at him. I'd practically attacked my burrito the moment it had been placed in front of me, and hadn't come up for air since. Looking around at the flamboyant walls of the small restaurant, I had to admit that Trace Walker stood out like a sore thumb. He'd asked me where I wanted to eat, and I'd directed him back to my neighborhood, an area that didn't have the finest of restaurants and was located in one of the most crime-ridden areas in the city. I couldn't help smiling as I looked at the gorgeous man across from me in a custom suit, seated at a rickety table covered in a well-used plastic table cloth.

He didn't belong here.

But I did.

"It's the best Mexican food in the city." The restaurant was family owned, and the food was fantastic. What did it matter that there was no fine china or fancy furnishings?

I watched as he practically inhaled the daily special, a look of appreciation on his face.

He nodded. "It's good. How did you ever find this place?"

I shrugged. "I live right around the corner."

Trace frowned, putting his fork down on his nearly-empty plate. "In this neighborhood? It's dangerous, especially at night."

I wouldn't know the difference between a good neighborhood and a bad one. This was home to me. "It's not so bad." I knew I sounded defensive, but it irked me that he was being uppity about a neighborhood I'd lived in for years.

"You're coming home with me. Your job starts now." He gave me a look that said he wouldn't change his mind.

I sighed. "Might as well. I'm being evicted anyway." My situation was dire, and I didn't like telling a man like Trace Walker what a loser I was, but it was the truth.

His expression was stormy as he picked up his fork and started eating again. "I'll call a mover to get your stuff."

"No need. I can just swing by and pick up my things. I don't own much." It was an understatement, but I tried to be nonchalant. Everything I had could fit in a backpack. I lived in a studio apartment, and it was sparsely furnished with things I'd been able to get for free. What clothing I had fit into my tattered backpack.

"Jesus! Who cares for you, Eva? Where are your parents? How long have you been on your own?"

"Nobody cares for me. I'm an adult, and I've been on my own since I was seventeen. My father was a Mexican born farm worker who died when I was fourteen years old, and my mother remarried and moved away when I was seventeen. She's dead now."

I didn't want to think about my parents, my family. I still missed my father, even though he'd been gone for nearly a decade. My mother was a different story. I'd hated her and the feelings were mutual before she'd died. I had plenty of reasons to harbor resentment and anger toward my mother. Making me and my father feel like dirt on her shoes was just one of them.

Trace placed his fork on his now-empty plate. "So you're Mexican?"

"Half," I corrected. "My mother was Caucasian American. I was born here."

To be honest, we'd traveled a lot within the U.S. up until my father had died. He went where there was work on the farms, and my mother and I had gone with him. Mom had constantly complained about the dirty, squalid life my dad provided, but he'd always worked long, hard hours out in the fields to keep us fed.

Sometimes I wondered why my mother had married my father. My childhood had been nothing but listening to her criticizing him for their poverty. Nevertheless, my father had never stopped trying to please her.

Unfortunately, he'd never made her happy, even when he'd died trying to keep our family intact. She'd been bitter about my existence keeping her trapped in the same place until the day she'd left to seek out a different kind of life, leaving me—and apparently all of those bad memories—behind.

My father had loved me; my mother had hated me.

Maybe I'd made peace with the fact that I wasn't responsible for my mother's unhappiness. But occasionally her bitter words still haunted me.

"Why were you left on your own when your mother remarried?"

Trace's question made me uncomfortable. "I was an adult, graduating from high school. She was done with her obligations to me."

Trace's eyes turned glacial. "A seventeen-year-old living here isn't equipped to live her own life yet."

Apparently, my mother had thought differently. She'd left me with more than just overdue bills and an eviction notice.

I looked at the man defending me, and all of the misplaced anger I'd carried for all of the Walkers faded. What had happened had nothing to do with the Walker family and everything to do with only one person: my mother.

"I made it. It doesn't matter." Nobody had ever cared about me enough to actually be angry that my life had been difficult. But for some reason, I didn't want Trace's pity.

"Barely," Trace grumbled as he stood up. "Let's get out of here."

I shoveled the last of my burrito into my mouth as I watched him pay the bill, giving the waitress a generous tip and a charismatic smile.

God, he was charming when he wasn't growling. I watched as he complimented the Hispanic waitress in fluent Spanish, letting her know how much he'd enjoyed the food. Somehow, it didn't surprise me that he could speak a foreign language so perfectly. He looked like the type of guy who did everything well.

Looking at his empty plate across from me, he was probably telling the truth about liking the food, even though he obviously wasn't impressed with the atmosphere.

His eyes shot back to me, still chewing the last of my burrito. I was full, but I'd be damned if I was going to leave one bite of food on my plate. When a person doesn't know when they'll eat again, leaving food when they have it seems almost criminal. I swallowed hard as his molten green eyes seemed to be urging me to move. Trace held out his hand, and I hesitated for a moment before I reached out and clasped it. I was on my feet with a single tug of his strong arm, which was attached to a very hard body.

My breath caught, the feel of his palm caressing mine sending shivers of longing through my body. How long had it been since I'd had the intimacy of a simple touch? How long had it been since someone had looked at me with such focused attention?

I was both relieved and disappointed when he looked away and started pulling me gently toward the door.

When we were back in his fancy black sports car, I gave him directions to my place, cringing as I led him up the creaky stairs to my second floor apartment.

He didn't comment as I gathered up my clothing and left my key on the small kitchen counter.

"I'll settle up with the landlord later," he remarked, his arm propped against the doorway, waiting.

"You're paying me. I'll take care of it." I sounded defensive, but I couldn't help it. I didn't want him dealing with my landlord or any of my other responsibilities.

"You're on the job, now. Didn't I say you follow my orders?" His voice was husky and firm.

"Not when it comes to my personal life." I was starting to get irritated.

"This job *is* personal."

I slung my backpack over my shoulder and glared at him. "Look, I want this job. I need it. But you said yourself that this was strictly business. Other than a job and payment, you have no right to interfere in my life. Teach me what you want me to know, how you want me to act, how you want me to look, and I'll do it. But managing the rest of my life isn't part of the deal."

"And if I think you need someone to manage your life?" His question was surly. "It doesn't look like you've done all that well doing it yourself so far."

Anger surged to the surface as I thought about every dirty, difficult job I'd had in my short working life. I'd survived any way I could. "What the hell would you know about survival?" I spat out at him. "Like you really understand what it's like to be a woman like me? I've worked my ass off since I was old enough to have a job. Do you think I *want* to be this way? Do you think I *want* to have to beg for employment, for food?" I took a deep tremulous breath, trying to control my rage. "No doubt you were handed everything you needed, went to an Ivy League college. I'm sure you started with at least a couple of billionaire dollars, a hard beginning for you." My voice grew louder and was dripping with sarcasm. "I'm sure you've never wondered whether you'd be better off dead than to keep trying to survive."

I'd been down that road so many times that I couldn't remember how many times I had contemplated the fact that not a single living soul would miss me if I no longer existed.

Trace moved so quickly that I didn't see him coming. He grasped me by the shoulders and shoved my backpack to the floor, then quickly pinned me against the wall next to the door. "Have you wondered that, Eva?"

I didn't speak. I was still reeling from the shock of his lightning fast movements.

"Tell me, dammit. Have you thought about that?"

His eyes were like heated liquid jade as they bored into mine. Hyperventilating, I glared at him defiantly, and I suddenly choked back an exhausted sob. I was tired, so tired of killing myself just to stay alive, but the survivor in me would never stop fighting.

He grasped a handful of my inky curls; my hair had come loose in our struggle. "You have considered it," he concluded from my lack of response. "Don't ever think like that again. Never. I don't like hearing you talk that way."

A single tear escaped my eye as I answered. "I'm sorry, Mr. Walker, but not everything revolves around what you like or want. Life's hard, and it stays that way."

I'd learned that even if it was possible to survive, happiness could be elusive and fleeting. When my father was alive, I'd been happy during the rare times we'd had together, just the two of us. I'd had a small taste of happiness during those outings. Other than that, I had little experience with joy.

"It should never have been this hard for you, Eva. You're right, I was born to privilege, but contentment can be just as difficult for everybody. Life is hard, no matter how much money you have." Trace's tone was even as he continued to stare, but the anger was still there. "The problems are just different."

I contemplated his words for a moment as I lowered my head and panted against his chest anxiously, wondering if there wasn't a little bit of truth to them. True, he didn't have to struggle for money, but Trace Walker was far from happy. Beneath his anger, I could sense his pain. Maybe he was right. Maybe life wasn't perfect just because he had food to eat, amazing vehicles to drive, and custom clothing to wear. Still, he'd never walked in my beat-up shoes, and I'd never walked in his custom loafers.

"Let's call a truce," I said breathlessly. "We come from two different worlds. We'll never understand each other."

I needed to get out of his hold. I was starting to get drunk on his masculine scent, and mesmerized by his ferocious gaze. He was big, powerful, and I had to tilt my head to look at his face.

He moved back slightly, only to place a hand on each side of my face gently before he said hoarsely, "I think we can communicate perfectly."

I opened my mouth to ask him to release me, but he was too stealthy and quick, his head lowering to capture my mouth in a demanding encounter that left me helpless and stunned.

He tilted my head, obtaining better access to my mouth, his tongue easily gaining entrance and commanding more.

More. More. More.

My heart stuttered as I wrapped my arms around his neck, my body coming alive as he pressed closer, pushed deeper, the kiss hot and all-consuming. I felt myself starting to drown in the scent of him, the taste of him, wanting to get closer, feel him invade my senses even deeper.

He wrenched his mouth away, cursing. "Fuck! I shouldn't have done that."

Trace sounded angrier with himself than he was with me. He rested his forehead on my shoulder, his breathing ragged. My heart was still racing as I realized that he had one hand on my ass, pressing my core against him, and his other arm around my back.

He didn't move to release me, and I didn't try to get away. I savored the feel of him, my body pressed so tightly against his larger form. Drawing a breath, I let his essence flow over me like a soothing balm to my soul.

Finally, I asked, "Why did you do that?"

"Because I couldn't control myself. Dammit!" He drew back and released his grip. "I don't lose control. Ever."

He sounded irritated and underneath that anger, slightly confused.

I'd never been the object of any man's lust, and it was slightly heady. Still, I couldn't figure out what he saw in *me*. Trace probably had most of the female population at his disposal. Why would he waste time on me when he could be nailing a supermodel?

"Sex isn't part of this deal," I told him shakily, part of me wishing that it was. But it would be wrong for so many reasons. Like it or not, this had to stay business only for me. Anything more could be a disaster, and I'd had enough of broken dreams and shattered hopes.

Running a frustrated hand through his hair, he answered, "I know that. I'm not looking for a damn prostitute."

I recoiled like he'd physically struck me. "I've never done...that."

His fierce gaze locked with mine, and his eyes devoured me.

"I know you haven't." Trace's voice was clipped and slightly pained. "I'm not about to hire a hooker to be my fiancée. No matter how well she played the part, my brothers would figure out the truth. Like I said, I need someone convincing."

"I have a part to play, but I'm not sleeping with you." Oh, but I wanted to. If that was a little taste of Trace, I wanted the feast. Unfortunately, I couldn't gorge. Not with him.

A cocky smirk formed on his lips. "Okay. But I'll still try to make you want me. I guarantee it."

I already wanted him. It was physically impossible for my body not to respond to a man like him.

I propped my hands on my hips. "Why?"

"Because I want *you*, Eva. I want my cock to be buried so deep inside you that you can't remember your own name, and you beg me to make you come." His tone was matter-of-fact, but his eyes were still burning green fire.

I slammed my eyes closed, not wanting to visualize that scenario. The effort was unsuccessful. "Not happening." I opened my eyes again.

"We'll see." Trace was still smiling, his expression decidedly smug.

"Besa mi culo." The insult telling him to kiss my ass in Spanish slipped from my lips before I could stop it.

"Bare it, and I'll kiss more than just your gorgeous ass," he promised dangerously.

Damn! I couldn't even insult him in Spanish because he'd understand every word.

Remembering his powerful grip on my ass, I flushed as my core clenched hard, as though my body was begging me to let him take me. He'd been hard, his cock straining against the confines of his pristine suit pants.

"Not happening." I tried to sound firm, but to my ears, I was even less convincing than the last time I'd said those same words. Truth was, I wasn't sure what I'd do if he really pushed my boundaries.

Luckily, I didn't have to find out.

He put my backpack over his shoulder easily, a burden that had almost made me crumble from the weight.

Trace didn't say another word as he motioned me out the door of my apartment.

"Do you have another key?" He glanced at me questioningly.

Digging into the zipper pocket of the backpack, I removed the spare key and locked the apartment door, and then put it in the back pocket of my jeans.

"I'll have fun retrieving that so I can deal with your landlord," Trace said with a smile in his voice.

Instantly, I reached into my pocket again, grabbed the key, and promptly shoved it under the door. "No, you won't." I smiled at him smugly.

He shrugged. "That won't stop me. But it does kill all the fun."

Trace's gaze was teasing, and I found it hard to resist a smiling Trace. I had a feeling it was something he didn't do often. "If you do, I'll quit."

"No, you won't." The certainty in his voice was annoying.

Nope. I probably wouldn't. Now that my apartment was gone, I needed a job to survive. My nose simply tilted up and I rolled my eyes at him. I stomped off to make my way back down the decrepit staircase.

He was right behind me. "Your Latina temper is pretty hot." His voice was gruff.

Shoving my nose further into the air, I huffed. "You haven't seen just how hot I can burn." I didn't lose my temper often. I couldn't afford to give it free reign whenever I wanted. But when I was really angry, I could fly off the handle with a lot more of a temper than he'd just seen.

I should have expected his retort; I should have known he'd pick up on the chance to make my defiant comment sexual. My words were going to have to be more closely monitored around him.

"I can't wait," he answered smoothly.

Since I had no answer, I hurried down the stairs, the sound of Trace's wicked laughter following me.

Bastard!

Part of me enjoyed his teasing, the sexual tension that flowed heavily between us. But I couldn't let it continue. I knew something he didn't, something that would instantly stop this budding part of our relationship that neither one of us could seem to control.

He has a right to know.

I swung around at the bottom of the stairs, almost colliding with Trace as he reached the ground floor.

"We can't do this." My voice was adamant and sad.

"I'm attracted to you, Eva," he answered candidly.

"You shouldn't be."

"Why not? You're an attractive woman."

I took a deep breath, unable to meet his eyes. I looked at the dirty wall with peeling white paint behind him. "I came to see you today for a favor. I was desperate. You don't know me, but I know of you. My mother left me to marry your father. Even though I never saw her again and we've never met, we're still related by marriage. Technically, you're my stepbrother."

CHAPTER THREE

Trace

I should have known from the moment I laid eyes on her that Eva Morales was trouble. No, correction...actually, her name was Evangelina Guadalupe Morales, something I'd learned from the papers I'd signed for her landlord.

She'd been pretty pissed when she'd found out I'd settled her rent, and as far as I knew, she was *still* angry. I was sitting in my home office doing some research after she had stormed off in the general direction of her bedroom about an hour earlier, her nose in the air and nearly palpable steam emanating from her body.

I've already admitted to myself that I enjoyed making her angry just to watch her heated reactions. But it played hell with my cock. Maybe it was sick and twisted, but the hotter she got, the more I wanted to subdue her, use that passion she had in a much better, more satisfying way for both of us.

Did I give a shit if she was angry?

No.

I'd become accustomed to getting what I wanted, and I had *needed* to take care of her for some unknown reason, and it wasn't because of some asinine attachment we had because her mother had supposedly married my father. Someone sure as hell needed to help manage Eva's life, and I'd already decided that person was going to be *me*. My desire to make her safe and happy was far from brotherly; it was a primitive, far more intimate, gut-wrenching need, one I didn't quite understand myself.

For the life of me, I couldn't figure out what attracted me to her, but my cock had been stiff since the moment I caught my first glimpse of her, and it had stayed that way. She'd put on a brave front, but I had still been able to spot her discomfort yesterday in my office, sense her vulnerability. The desire to strip her naked and nail her up against a wall, on my desk, or any other solid surface had hit me almost immediately. But as badly as I had wanted to fuck her, every instinct I had insisted that I also...keep her safe.

Those two primal desires were waging war inside me, and even I wasn't sure which one was going to win.

The fact that she was technically my stepsister hadn't dulled my desire to fuck her until she screamed my name in climax at all. Maybe that showed I was a total prick, but I didn't care.

We weren't even remotely blood related, and I hadn't known that my stepmother had borne a daughter. But then, how much had any of us known about Karen? She had died almost immediately, along with my father, after their marriage. The private jet carrying my brother, Dane, my father, and Dad's new wife - Eva's mother - had crashed. Dane, my youngest sibling, had been the only survivor.

Dane had barely come through the experience alive, and my concern for him was the only reason I had to, *needed* to, have a woman I was committed to by Christmas. My youngest brother was still scarred, inside and out, from his near-fatal crash, and there wasn't much I wouldn't do to keep him from going over the edge.

The sound of a ringing phone on the desk jarred me from thoughts, my eyes flying to the caller ID.

Sebastian.

The bastard hadn't called me in over a month, probably avoiding the lecture he knew he'd get if he phoned. My middle brother was getting wild, hanging out with a bunch of losers. I'd tried to give him time to find his own direction after the accident that had killed our father, but even though he was now a few years out of college, it appeared he had no moral compass.

I snatched up the ringing phone impatiently. "Where in the fuck have you been?"

"Well, hell, I miss you, too, bro," Sebastian answered sarcastically.

Dammit! I could tell he was either drunk or stoned, beyond the point where I could even talk to him. "Working. Something you don't seem inclined to do." My voice was clipped and angry.

I was pissed off, and I was done making excuses for Sebastian. He needed to grow the fuck up.

"Why should I when I have you to be the perfect, responsible brother who has everything under control? You're a fucking god, bro. No need to have two of them in the family." Sebastian's voice was slightly slurred and filled with antagonistic sarcasm.

Sebastian wasn't always this way, but the instances where he seemed inclined to irritate me were becoming more and more frequent. "When are you flying in for the holidays? Dane is going to be here the week before Christmas." I didn't feel like engaging with him in a verbal battle, not when he was like this. It was pointless.

My brother seemed to sober up slightly. "I'll get there around the same time. I haven't seen Dane for a while."

Releasing the tight fist I was clenching on the desk, I remembered that at one time the three of us had been pretty tight. After the accident, things had never been quite the same. Dane was profoundly different, Sebastian had grown away from everybody in the family, and I had become a major prick because I had to run my father's business, something I hadn't been prepared for at such a young age.

"Are you bringing anyone?" I needed to figure out sleeping arrangements, but I was mostly curious as to whether Sebastian was seriously involved with a female. Considering the crowd he was running with right now, I was hoping he wasn't.

"Nope. I'm flying solo." Sebastian paused for a moment before asking, "You? Have you found a woman who will put up with your cranky ass for more than an hour?"

Not so long ago, I would have told Sebastian everything. Now, I didn't trust him. He ran hot and cold these days, and the last thing I needed was for Dane to find out the truth. "As a matter of fact, I have. Congratulate me. I'm recently engaged."

I waited as the line was silent, knowing Sebastian was still connected, but wasn't talking.

Finally, he answered. "You got engaged? And you didn't say anything? I didn't even know you were seeing anyone."

Fuck! Now I was feeling guilty because there was an underlying hurt in my brother's voice. It made me feel like a complete asshole, but there was more at stake than just Sebastian's feelings.

I can't tell him. He's too unpredictable.

"Whirlwind relationship. You'll like her," I told him awkwardly, knowing I was a shitty liar when it came to fabrications with my brothers. Most people didn't know the me who lay beneath my professional demeanor. Hell, I barely knew myself anymore.

"What's she like? Where did you meet her? Do I know her?" Sebastian was quickly sobering up.

"Nice. No. And no, you don't know her." I answered his questions rapidly, hoping he'd let the subject go.

"What's her name?" Sebastian persisted.

"Eva." I decided to keep it simple. He'd be meeting her soon enough, and I was uncomfortable talking about her.

Did it matter if Eva was technically *their* stepsister? Should *they* know the truth? I didn't see why they should. They'd never known, and they'd never met her. She wasn't blood, so there wasn't much harm in keeping our flimsy ties a secret. Hell, I hadn't even completely verified her claim yet, but I was already working on that. I did know that even when I did have proof that she was really our stepsister, I wouldn't tell them. Dane could never know the truth.

"Do you love her?" Sebastian sounded puzzled.

Jesus Christ! I hated lying to him, even though he'd been a fucking jerk for a while now. "Yes." The word slipped from my mouth easily, the lie complete by uttering one single word.

"Damn. She must be hot."

"She's smart, kind, and honest." I said those words without even thinking, knowing them to be the truth. Eva was everything many women in our circles were not. Maybe that was why I had this unholy instinct to fuck her and protect her at the same time.

"I notice you didn't say she was hot," Sebastian mumbled.

"Touch her and I swear I'll put you in the hospital," I growled, unable to stop visions of Sebastian acting inappropriately with Eva.

"Holy shit, bro. I think you really are in love. And she really must be beautiful. I might be a dick, but you know I'd never touch another man's woman, especially my brother's." There was some anger in Sebastian's voice.

Yeah, I knew that. Sebastian had good reason to be testy about the subject. "I know." *But when you're intoxicated, you're a different person from the brother I knew and trusted.* I didn't add those thoughts to our conversation.

"Is Dane bringing Britney?"

I recoiled at the mention of *her* name, not because she meant a damn thing to me anymore, but because Dane was, in fact, bringing the woman I'd once cared about. Neither of my brothers knew I'd been intimate with Britney—in the biblical sense, or why she was now pretending she was madly in love with Dane. I knew she didn't love my brother because she wasn't capable of love. Britney was a user, a manipulator.

"He's bringing her," I replied flatly.

"Now there's one hot woman," Sebastian whistled appreciatively.

Britney was beautiful, but as attractive as a poisonous snake to me now. "On the surface, perhaps she is."

"Are you jealous?" Sebastian's voice was more quizzical than teasing.

"No. But I don't trust that she's with Dane for the right reasons." I wanted Sebastian to see the truth for himself since I couldn't tell him.

"You think she's jerking his chain? That she only cares about his money?" Sebastian's voice became clearer, and slightly hesitant.

"I guess we'll figure that out eventually." I was noncommittal because I needed to be. "But I don't trust her."

"You know something I don't, Trace?"

"No. It's just instinct," I lied.

"The last thing Dane needs is more pain," Sebastian grumbled. "But it makes sense. Dane is scarred, and it's going to take a good woman to look beyond that to see who he really is."

I wished Sebastian hadn't been telling the truth, but he was. And Dane needed a far better woman than blood-sucking Britney. "We'll see what happens." My youngest brother was a far better man than either me or Sebastian. Kinder, gentler, at least he had been in the past.

My plan was to get Britney out of Dane's life without causing him any heartache, but I wasn't certain that was possible.

"I gotta go, bro. I ducked out of a party, but there's a good whiskey calling my name."

Dammit! I'd do anything to keep Sebastian from drinking himself into oblivion, and a sense of helplessness invaded my gut because of the physical and emotional distance between us. I didn't want him driving, didn't want him to get himself killed. Yeah, he was an adult and a dick most of the time, but he was still my brother. "Sebastian, you don't have to do this. Where are you?"

"Don't start with the bullshit tonight, Trace. I just wanted to hear your voice."

The last thing I wanted was to be my brother's conscience or his moral guide. Fuck, I knew I wasn't qualified. I just wanted him to be okay. I wanted *all of us* to be okay.

Truth was, I wanted to hear his voice, too, and I wanted my damn family back.

"See ya in a few weeks." Sebastian disconnected, and I was left with very few options but to hope I could talk sense into him when he got here.

After slamming the phone back into the charger, frustrated, I got up just as the doorbell rang.

I smiled as I moved toward the door, knowing more deliveries were here, knowing I was going to piss Eva off all over again—if she'd ever gotten over the first time.

Thinking about it, I didn't care. I'd rather see her angry than looking lost, alone or scared.

I was more than ready to be preoccupied with Eva and her protests.

Ultimately, I knew I would win.

I always did.

CHAPTER FOUR

Eva

*I*t really annoyed me that Trace Walker thought I wasn't capable of taking care of myself. Granted, it might look that way from his perspective, but now that I was going to have a job, a chance at a better life, I'd be fine.

As long he never finds out...

Abruptly, I banished the negative thought from my mind. He'd made a promise, and he wouldn't break it. I hoped.

I had been upset when he'd told me he'd taken care of my landlord after I asked him not to do it. I had money now, his check safely deposited in my checking account. I was perfectly capable of taking care of my own problems.

We'd argued about the money, too, but he'd insisted on me taking the offered pay of twenty-five thousand up front, and I'd finally decided to just take it. I could give him back what I didn't need once this farce was over.

Somehow I need to find a way to stop arguing with him!

Maybe if he wasn't such an arrogant, highhanded dick, we could get along.

I smiled just a little, admitting to myself that his arrogance fueled my temper. Not that I hadn't met conceited men, but not one quite like *him*. Even in his most pompous and audacious moments, he was thinking about my welfare. It didn't completely deflate me, but it made it damn hard to hate him.

Trace Walker was used to being obeyed. Being bossy was obviously in his DNA.

"You look amazing, darling," a low, female voice crooned, the voice of my new stylist.

I actually have a stylist for God's sake.

Claudette was superficial, but pleasant enough to be around. I guessed she was probably in her sixties, but she was brilliantly put together, not one dark hair out of place. She was sporting a chic business look that I hoped I could pull off some day.

She stopped fussing with the red cocktail dress I was trying on, and I turned to look in the full length mirror in my assigned bedroom, still not used to being in a place so enormous and elegant.

I'd spent my first night in Trace's expansive home wandering around in a daze, almost getting lost in the process, before I finally collapsed on the beautiful sleigh bed in this bedroom, a space that Trace nonchalantly assigned as my quarters for the time being.

I froze as my eyes caught my reflection, looking back at an image I barely recognized.

My hair had been trimmed into a sleek style that left it curling around my shoulders. Claudette had worked some kind of magic with carefully applied makeup, and explained how to do it myself. The dress, that ended in a sophisticated swirl right below my knees, had tight long sleeves that clung to my arms like a second skin, and left most of my back bare. It wasn't a style I was used to wearing, and I'd never felt so naked in something that was long-sleeved.

"It's...nice." I could barely keep myself from gaping.

I looked like a different woman; I felt like a different woman.

"You look beautiful, Eva." Trace spoke low and husky from the doorway of my bedroom.

I turned to him, my eyes meeting his after he assessed me carefully. My body started to burn beneath his heated stare.

"Thanks. But I don't really think I need this many clothes." I nearly tripped on my matching high heels as I stepped back from the mirror to face him.

I'd been hooked up with a complete wardrobe. Claudette was taking back the items she hadn't liked; unfortunately, she liked far too many of them.

Trace looked at Claudette. "Thank you. I think you're finished here."

The older woman nodded and started to walk toward the door, skirting around Trace. "I'll have my staff pick up the equipment and the clothes that weren't appropriate later, Mr. Walker." She left hurriedly, knowing she had been dismissed.

Trace lifted his brow. "The clothes are part of the deal."

I propped my hands on my hips. "Not this many of them. Where am I going to wear this kind of dress?"

He shrugged. "Parties. I have a corporate Christmas party to attend this year, and I need you to be there. I told you that this needs to be believable."

My heart raced at the thought of being on Trace's arm for *any* event. Just being in his company made me edgy. "You still haven't told me why."

I let go of my earlier anger, telling myself I needed to treat this as a job.

Trace moved into my bedroom - which was twice the size of my studio apartment, I might add - and sat down on the oversized ledge of the window seat.

I toed off my heels and moved to the bed. I sat in the middle of the enormous beige and floral quilt and crossed my legs, pulling the skirt over them. I could sense he was going to tell me something important, and I stayed silent.

Trace propped a strong shoulder against the wall. "You know that your mother and my father died in a plane crash?"

I nodded. I knew how my mother had met her demise soon after her wedding to Trace's father.

"My youngest brother was on board that private jet, too, and he survived...just barely. He was burned and scarred, and even with plastic surgery, he still has scars inside and out." He paused for a moment and then continued, "I was supposed to be on that plane with them, but I had final exams. I was graduating from college. I had to leave as soon as the ceremony was over. So did my middle brother, Sebastian. Dane was the only one whose classes and exams had ended because he was at a different school, so he stayed a few more days."

Oh, God. My stomach knotted at the thought that Trace could be dead instead of so very much alive. I gaped at him, still able to feel his vitality and energy vibrating through the bedroom. I could also feel his tension. "It bothers you that you weren't on that plane. You feel guilty."

Trace didn't show his hand with his expression, but I was close enough to see a look of pain flash briefly in his eyes.

"I don't wish myself dead," he snapped. "But the fact that it should have been me did cross my mind."

He was so responsible, so damned ready to take on the entire world. "It wouldn't have made a difference."

His fists clenched and he shot me an irritated stare. "How do I know that? Maybe I could have gotten Dane out of the wreckage quicker, maybe I could have prevented the surgeries he's had, so damn many that I've lost count."

My heart bled for the man who thought he could prevent all the hurts in the world. I'd learned that I had to pick my battles. He obviously hadn't. "And maybe you'd be dead. Maybe you would have blocked people from getting him out. Everybody else on the plane died that day, including the pilot. Do you think you're invincible?" I shot back at him, trying to make him see what was most likely true: whether he'd been on that plane or not wouldn't have changed the outcome.

His lips twitched, probably because of my annoyed tone, but I wasn't certain.

"So you think my dead body would have gotten him dead, too?"

I shrugged. "It might have gotten in the way."

"Comforting thought." His tone was sarcastic, but there was a trace of amusement there, too.

Not wanting to think about him not being alive, I prompted, "Go on."

Trace released a low, resigned sigh. "Dane has been through a lot, emotionally and physically. He's recently started dating a woman who I'm well acquainted with. She's seeing him to get back at me, and she's hoping I'll take her back. I ended our association over a year ago because she wasn't satisfied with just me. She was bed hopping with every wealthy man in Colorado."

"Stupid woman," I said without thinking. But really, why would any female need another man when she had Trace Walker. "I'm sorry. I'm sure you were faithful to her."

He grinned at me, and my heart melted. He nodded and said, "I was. I wasn't ready to make a big commitment, but we had dated long enough that she finally talked me into a monogamous relationship. Too bad she meant only on my side."

"You still love her?" My palms were sweaty and my heart started to hammer. I wasn't quite sure I wanted his answer.

"I never said I loved her. I just said we were supposed to be exclusive. I don't love, Eva. I satisfy a physical need with the women I see."

It was pretty obvious that he did much more than that. Oh, he might not have ever been in love, but the way he cared about his brother told me he was capable. "So you need me as a decoy?"

"I need you to keep her away from me. Dane would be devastated if he knew all that Britney wanted were the things his money can buy her, and she's getting back at me."

"Maybe she really does care now. Maybe things have changed," I said, hopeful that Britney may have had an epiphany.

How could any woman be so heartless to use brother against brother, especially one who had suffered like Dane?

"She called me just a few weeks ago, telling me that she was hoping to win me back at Christmas. She hasn't changed." His voice was flat and hopeless. "I want Dane to dump her. She's a viper. But not because she was making moves on me. I don't want him to resent me, or to know that I fucked her first."

I hated that thought, the idea that Trace had done the horizontal mambo with *any* female. Unfortunately, I was pretty sure he'd done a lot of bedroom dancing.

"I'll do my best," I promised him. "But you're going to have to help me. Pretend that you care."

"I won't have to pretend, Eva. If I didn't want you to have a better life, I wouldn't have chosen you. I could have found someone else, but you were just too damn perfect. You're very beautiful."

He was wrong. I was a loser in a gorgeous dress. "I feel like Cinderella," I mumbled before I could stop myself. The room was silent for a minute before I added, "What are we doing here together if they aren't coming until Christmas? Tomorrow is Thanksgiving."

"I'm well aware of that. I thought I'd take you out for dinner. The time won't be wasted. I can get you through our pre-employment process and fill you in on details."

"I'll cook. I want to," I said eagerly. It had been years since I'd participated in a Thanksgiving dinner.

His eyes stared at me, penetrating me with an intense gaze. "You actually want to cook?"

"Your kitchen is amazing. And yes, I love to cook. I just haven't had a chance in a very long time." I'd never had the money. Lately, I hadn't had a scrap of food in my apartment. "Do you have the supplies?"

He frowned. "Probably not. And I gave my staff time off now until next Monday. But I can call my assistant here."

I held up a hand. "No. Don't you have a car?"

He smirked. "Several of them."

"You can drive me. I'm not driving one of those fancy, expensive vehicles of yours." Knowing my luck, I'd crash.

"To a grocery store?" He looked appalled.

"Really? You act like you never get groceries."

He shrugged. "I don't. I have employees for that."

"Then it will be an adventure, right?" I couldn't fathom somebody who had his shopping done for him, but all I needed was a ride. "I know what to get. I'll check out your kitchen to see what you already have."

I scooted off the bed, ready to get out of the fancy dress I was wearing. It made me feel pretty, but also like someone that wasn't really...me.

Trace stood up. "You don't have to do this, Eva. I don't mind shoving something in the microwave or going out."

"It's Thanksgiving. You can't eat a frozen dinner." If it hadn't been for Trace, I wouldn't be eating at all. I wanted to do this for him. "Just give me a few minutes to change." I nudged him toward the door.

"Can I watch?" he asked mischievously.

His molten green gaze caressed me, and I swear I could feel his stare all the way down to my toes. My core clenched painfully as I caught his scent.

"Leave, pervert," I insisted.

He turned toward me, stopping as he said, "I'll be downstairs."

"I'll be ready in a few minutes. I just need to get out of this dress."

I swore I heard him groan before he caught me in his arms, one hand behind the small of my back, and the other wrapping around the nape of my neck. "You're killing me, Eva."

His mouth met mine with a single-minded determination that I'd never experienced before. His kiss was hot, all-consuming, and I felt myself going under and caving in almost immediately.

Something about Trace drew me to him, and I kissed him back, opening beneath his demanding mouth as his tongue commanded entry. I sighed against his lips and put my arms around his neck, letting him take what he wanted because I knew I wanted the same thing.

Desire shot through my body like an electrical current as he moved his hand down to my ass and pulled my moist core up and against his swollen cock.

I want him inside me.

I need him inside me.

I resented the clothing that separated our bodies.

He didn't know anything about me, but he wanted me. I was getting drunk on passion, lost in the way he kissed me like he *had* to, *needed* to, or he couldn't draw another breath.

Tapping into Trace's need was a euphoric feeling, the fact that a woman like me could cause someone like him to kiss me with this kind of desire was as heady as it got.

I knew we had to stop. My nipples hardened as he pulled me closer, my sensitive breasts abrading the jacket of his suit.

Still, he kept on touching me, the hand that was previously behind my neck now fisting in my hair.

My voice was breathless, my eyes closed as his mouth stopped ravaging mine and moved to the sensitive skin of my neck. "Oh, God. Trace. Please stop." I knew that I sure as hell couldn't separate myself from him. I wanted to hold on, let him take me as far as I could go.

"Eva. I want you so damn much," he rasped into my ear.

"I want you, too. But I can't do this." He was my stepbrother, but it wasn't that knowledge that stopped me. We barely knew each other; the only thing we had in common was an incredible chemistry.

Finally, he released me. "We *can* do this, but I'll wait until you're ready." He sounded pained.

I'm ready. I'm so damn ready.

He backed away and my eyes fluttered open, the pain of losing contact with him excruciating.

"What are you afraid of, Eva?" he asked hoarsely.

I looked at him, at the molten heat in his eyes.

I'm afraid you'll hate me some day.

I'm afraid I'll become addicted to you, and I can't.

I'm afraid that once I'm intimate with you, I'll never want to let you go.

"I don't sleep around, especially not with my stepbrother." I wanted to tease him, but my voice was cracking with emotion.

He captured my chin and tilted it up. "The last thing I feel for you is brotherly affection," he told me angrily. "I want to fuck you so badly that I can hardly breathe. *You* want *me* to fuck you so badly that you can hardly breathe."

I was honest enough to admit I wanted the same thing, but it couldn't happen. "Please. I hardly know you." I wasn't sure if I was begging him to do me, or asking him to leave me alone.

In the end, he decided for me. "I'm going. But we'll get to know each other over the next few days. Guaranteed, I'll try to get you naked. And I'll succeed."

I shuddered at the thought, watching him, my body still trembling, every muscle tight with unspent desire. When he started down the stairs, I closed the bedroom door before I could allow myself to call him back to me.

CHAPTER FIVE

Trace

T hump!

Thump!

Thump, thump, thump!

"She's driving me fucking crazy," I rasped to myself as my padded gloves and bare feet kept making satisfying connections with the heavy punching bag suspended in front of me.

I'd been perfecting my MMA skills for years, but you'd never know it. My technique sucked right now, and I wasn't really practicing. I'd grabbed my gloves and pulled on a pair of grappling shorts. I hadn't bothered wrapping my hands. All I really wanted was to blow off steam, a hell of a lot of sexual energy that I couldn't seem to lose elsewhere. For me, that meant I needed to punch something.

Thump, thump, thump!

I'd been beating up the bag with everything I had for over fifteen minutes.

But my dick was still hard.

Thump!

My breath sawed in and out of my lungs, and sweat was trickling from my face and landing on my drenched chest, but I still wasn't spent. One glimpse of Eva in her *fuck-me* dress had done me in.

I'd barely made it out of her room without lifting the hem of her dress over her ass and taking her against the wall. Usually, that's exactly what I'd do. But the way I felt when I looked at her defied my usual reason.

I wanted her, but I also felt like I *needed* her. Experiencing emotions like that was foreign to me, and I didn't like it.

I fucked.

I sent nice gifts.

And I was done.

Britney was the only woman I'd ever had a monogamous relationship with, and look how shitty that had turned out. I'd never done exclusivity again, before or after my experience with the girlfriend-from-hell.

Strangely, I'd never been possessive of Britney or any other woman. I didn't think it was in my DNA. The only reason I'd gone exclusive with Britney was because *she* had wanted it, and I had been pretty ambivalent at the time. There hadn't been anyone else I wanted to fuck, and I was okay with her being the only one. Too bad she hadn't felt the same way, even though she'd been the one to insist on being my one and only.

Now, not only did I want to nail Eva until she couldn't walk, but I was also covetous of her, possessive for the first time in my life.

"Jesus! I'm pathetic," I growled, throwing random punches and kicks at the bag in front of me, breathing hard when I finally stopped.

Shucking the gloves as I headed toward the shower of my home gym, I knew Eva was probably ready and waiting upstairs for me to take her to the store.

I was feeling only slightly better as I got dressed after stroking myself to orgasm in the shower to fantasies of making Eva come in a variety of ways.

What in the fuck was happening to me? There was any number of women I could call, but that wasn't what I wanted, and it wasn't going to satisfy me any more than my own hand just did.

I climbed the stairs in a pair of jeans and a sweatshirt, almost certain I was completely losing my mind.

Watching Eva shop in a pair of skin-tight jeans and a sweater, obviously part of her new wardrobe judging by the designer label on the back pocket of the denim, was almost a sensual experience.

She clung to the food reverently, as though it were precious. When she stroked the damn turkey like it was some kind of grand prize, I wanted to come right there in the fucking grocery isle.

"Is that the one?" I asked impatiently, anxious to get her away from the turkeys.

She sighed, and I wanted to absorb the satisfied sound with my mouth over hers.

"It should work good. There's just the two of us. We'll be eating leftovers for days, even with this one." She hefted up what looked like an enormous bird to me, not that I knew anything about finding the right Thanksgiving turkey.

She looked happy, and so damn beautiful doing such a mundane task that I wanted to bottle her enthusiasm so I could get drunk on it later.

Moving forward, I tried to take the heavy item, but she refused.

I motioned for her to hurry up and add it to the cart. "Drop it in." *And get me the fuck out of here now.*

She didn't dump it in the cart. Eva placed it in the bottom carefully, moving other items around to make room. Then, she gave the plump bird another small pat. "I think that's it. We should be done. Your cupboards are well-stocked. You just didn't have a few of the things we needed for a Thanksgiving dinner."

I didn't cook. My employees knew that. Most of my dinners were ordered in or easy to heat. Until Eva, I'd never even wondered who shopped for me, or how exactly what I wanted seemed to magically appear in my cupboards.

I was close enough to smell her delicate, intoxicating scent, and when she looked up at me and smiled, I decided that I wanted to keep this woman happy no matter what I needed to do.

Mine.

I felt the word all the way to my gut. Eva didn't know it yet, but she belonged to me. At least for a little while.

"Eva?" A female voice squealed from down the aisle.

I watched as Eva turned around, her expression breaking into an even broader smile.

"Isa!" She ran to meet the woman halfway, the two females colliding in an awkward tangle of arms as they hugged happily.

"Where have you been? I was so worried when I couldn't get in touch with you."

The woman's voice lowered after that comment, and I casually strode closer to listen to their conversation.

Isa—whoever the person might be to Eva—was absolutely stunning. She was a little taller than Eva, but around the same age.

Eva turned to introduce her friend to me. "Isa, this is Trace Walker, my..." She seemed to be searching for words.

"Her fiancé," I finished, smiling at the pretty dark-haired female next to Eva. There was no way I wanted any of Eva's friends knowing the truth. Hell, not even my own brother was going to know.

"Trace, this is my friend, Isa Jones. We lost track of each other for a while. She ran off after she got married."

Isa playfully punched Eva's arm. "I didn't run off. You moved and I didn't know." She stuck out her hand. "It's very nice to meet you. I've heard a lot about you from the media."

The female had a strong, confident handshake, and she met my eyes directly. I liked that. It wasn't any big surprise that she knew of me. It seemed that I was everybody's favorite target for the gossip columns and magazines. I hated knowing that the Walker name was infamous, and that people I didn't know actually knew my name and selected information I chose to release. That part of being wealthy had never failed to bother me. I preferred that my private life stayed private, but that wasn't going to happen. It was something I'd accepted over the years as being a down side to having a lot of money. I didn't have much choice. I was born with the proverbial silver spoon in my mouth, and because I worked my ass off, my fortune only got larger.

"My pleasure." I put a charming smile on my face.

Stepping back, Isa asked, "How long have you been together?"

Seeing her discreet glance at Eva's ring finger, I knew *that* was a situation I had to rectify soon. She needed a ring.

"We've been...connected for years," Eva said carefully. "But we just made the big commitment. We haven't even had time to get a ring."

Eva was good, so good that even I almost believed her. She could tell the absolute truth, but make it vague without anyone suspecting there was more than what she was saying.

We've been...connected for years? Technically, she's my stepsister, so I guess that's true.

Guilt pounded at me for the dire circumstances Eva had suffered. Yeah, maybe I *hadn't* known I had a stepsister, but I'd never thought to ask. As far as I knew, my brothers didn't have a clue that Eva had existed either. My father had grown children, and Eva's mother hadn't been that much younger than my dad. It made sense that she had borne a child...now.

I reached out and clasped Eva's hand, only to find her fingers were like an iceberg.

"You cold?" I asked.

She squeezed my hand. "No. I'm fine."

It felt natural to keep her next to me. I didn't find out much more about Eva, but through the conversation, I did discover that Isa was married to a man I knew and admired, a wealthy technology genius.

Isa hugged Eva again. "Please don't lose touch. I've missed you, and I've wondered how your educational plans worked out."

I wondered what Eva had been planning, but I didn't ask. Somehow, I had a sense that she was uncomfortable talking to Isa about it. She'd lowered her head, and she was no longer looking her friend in the eye. Her body language was screaming that she was distressed.

"Do you have a cell phone?" I asked Isa, changing the focus of the conversation.

It was easy to presume, by the look in Eva's eyes, that she'd missed Isa, too, but just didn't want to talk about whatever her plans had been right now.

Isa rummaged in her purse and pulled out her phone.

"I'll put in Eva's new cell." I already knew the number by heart, which was both pathetic and normal for me. I was naturally good with numbers, and had perfect recall if the numbers were important enough for me to remember. The fact that my brain had subconsciously recorded the number of the cell phone I'd purchased for *Eva* was pretty sad. There were very few phone numbers I considered important, and all of those numbers were already in my phone, including hers. I'd put it in as soon as I'd purchased the phone and set it up. Strange that for some reason, I'd thought the number was important enough to take up space in my already overcrowded mind.

I handed the cell phone back to Isa after entering Eva's number.

The women hugged again, with a promise from both of them to call and catch up.

"She was important to you. Still is," I guessed as we walked toward the checkout.

"Yes." Eva's tone was guarded.

"A friend? She looks older than you."

"She was a teaching assistant at my high school. I'm guessing she's probably a teacher now. She was finishing up her teaching degree when we met." She paused before asking, "Since when do I have a cell phone?"

I ignored her question. I'd bought her plenty that she hadn't seen yet. "How did she end up married to Jones?" A teaching assistant and a tech mogul was an interesting combination.

Eva shrugged. "She was already dating him when I met her, so I'm not sure how they met. But she looks happy."

"So what were your plans?" That was actually what I was most curious about, and I raised a brow at her after unloading the groceries onto the belt. She was silent.

"Sometimes plans don't work out," she answered abruptly.

Something was wrong, I could sense it, recognizing the thread of sadness in her voice mingling with her defensiveness.

"You'll tell me when we get home." I'd wring it out of her somehow. I'd banish all of the shadows of her past because they irritated me. Eva was the type of woman who was inherently made to be happy, yet she'd somehow been robbed of the opportunity.

She got screwed by a selfish mother who hadn't given a shit about her.

The more I thought about it, the more it pissed me off. My dad had had expectations for all of his sons. He'd been a savvy businessman, and he'd been formidable, but he wasn't the type not to accept a new daughter had Eva's mother chosen to bring her into the family.

Eva was quiet as we exited the store, and that annoyed me even more. I had to know why she had been forgotten when her mother had taken off for Texas to marry my dad. Hell, she obviously hadn't even stayed for Eva's high school graduation. What kind of parent was that?

Seeing her apartment and how Eva had been living made my gut ache. Granted, I knew next to nothing about Karen Morales, but I was going to make it a point to find out.

My control was something I valued, and I was slowly losing it completely when it came to Eva. I needed to find out what was wrong so I could fix it. When I buried my cock inside her, I greedily wanted her complete attention.

I didn't want gratitude.

I didn't want her to feel like she owed me.

All I wanted was her pleasure, and those climatic moments would belong to me and only me.

If that made me a selfish bastard, I didn't care, but I *would* make her mine.

I had no doubt that I'd win.

I always do.

CHAPTER SIX

Eva

I prepared a brine to marinate the turkey, my mouth watering at the thought of our Thanksgiving feast tomorrow. I hadn't eaten regular meals in so long that the thought of eating a huge meal seemed almost decadent.

I knew Trace was waiting for me, wanting to pick up the conversation where we'd left off in the grocery store. Now that I'd stored the plump bird in the fridge, I had little reason to avoid him. Except for the fact that I really didn't want to talk about Isa or the dreams that I'd had right before I graduated from high school. That was a long time ago, and things had changed more than I ever dreamed possible...and not in a good way.

Release it. Let it go.

There was nothing I could do to change my past, but I could decide my own future now.

I was washing my hands way longer than I needed to when I heard a male voice right next to me. "Wine?" he asked, holding out a beautiful wine glass partially filled with white wine.

Not being much of a drinker, I had no idea what I liked when it came to alcohol. Nevertheless, I thought I could use a drink. I noted he was holding a small glass with something that looked stronger than the wine I took from his hand.

"Thanks," I answered gratefully, taking a careful sip of the pale liquid. "It's good."

"I wasn't sure what you liked."

I smiled at him weakly. "That makes two of us. I'm not sure either. I don't really drink alcohol much."

"Come sit with me. Are you done?"

I was, but I really wanted to tell him that I had a ton of things to do in the kitchen. But for some reason, I couldn't lie to him. "Yes."

He nodded his head toward the living room, and I followed. He'd turned on the enormous gas fireplace, and the room was so inviting. I'd discovered that although Trace liked quality, he wasn't one to blatantly flash his wealth. The neutral colors were lovely, the leather of the furniture butter-soft, but the room was still comfortable.

I took a seat in one of the leather recliners. He stretched out his large form on a matching sofa across from me.

He was still wearing the same pair of black jeans that hugged his body, and a green sweatshirt that matched his eyes. Jesus, he was gorgeous, his short hair slightly mussed, giving him a look that was almost...touchable.

Thank God he was sitting far enough away that I couldn't smell his unique masculine scent, but the short separation wasn't helping much. I still wanted to strip him naked and crawl up his body and beg him to fuck me.

"Tell me now, Eva. What were your plans back when you were getting out of high school?"

His baritone was rich and smooth, and it flowed over me like velvet.

I took a slug of my wine, knowing I would have to talk about some of my past. "When I was sixteen, I got a job in a restaurant. I learned a lot by working in the kitchen. I wanted to pursue a career in the culinary arts, and Isa helped me find an apprenticeship program. I could work and study at the same time. She did a lot of things that she didn't need to do, like helping me with arranging some financial aid and applying for scholarships. But as soon as I graduated, things changed."

Please don't ask me anymore. I'd told him everything I wanted to reveal.

"Changed how?"

I shrugged. "My mother left, and I had bills to pay."

"Her bills?"

"The rent was overdue, and I was going to be evicted. At the time, I had no idea where she'd gone. I had to give up every penny I'd saved to keep a roof over my head."

He frowned. "Why didn't she tell you, take you with her? My dad was strict, but he would have welcomed you. He wouldn't have wanted you to be left alone at seventeen. Christ! She just deserted you."

She'd done much more than that, but I wasn't going to tell him just how coldhearted my mother had been. What good would it do? "She hated my father, and she despised me. I reminded her of every failure she'd ever had in her life. Her marriage to my dad was one of her big ones, or so she said. I think she had to marry my father because he got her pregnant. My grandparents wouldn't accept him...or me." Lord knew I'd heard about how I ruined my mother's life often enough—her mixed-race child that her parents would never take in.

"Why?"

"He was a laborer, and we were always barely scraping by. But he kept us fed and put a roof over our head."

Trace looked at me sharply. "You cared about him. You miss him."

I nodded. "Every single day since he died. I loved him, and he loved me." I hadn't known the warmth of parental affection since the day my father had left this earth, and I think I'd always miss it.

"I never really knew Karen," Trace mused angrily. "None of us knew about you, Eva, or we would have come for you. Honestly, I only met your mother once, and that was at the wedding. All of us were surprised when we found out Dad was getting married. Sebastian and I were in college, and Dane was getting ready to leave, too. I guess Dad was lonely."

"Why would you feel obligated to help me? You aren't really family." The Walkers had no reason to rescue me. Granted, I'd harbored resentment toward anyone with the name Walker, but they'd been just as faultless as I was.

"Because none of us are like your late mother," he growled, sitting his drink on the table and standing up.

He grasped my hand and pulled me over on the couch with him. The wine still balanced in my hand, I sat reluctantly, letting him pull me closer to his body. I wanted to be there, but I didn't. His scent filled my senses; his nearness made me want things I could never have.

I sighed as he took my wine glass and set it on the table next to his empty tumbler. For a moment, I let my body sink into his larger form, letting myself believe that he would have helped me, protected me, after my mother had left.

His arms tightened around me, and I laid my head on his shoulder. Tears leaked from the corners of my eyes because he felt so damn good. It had been so long since anyone had actually cared about me.

"Thank you. It's not your fault that you didn't know."

"I didn't ask, and I hate myself for that."

Tilting my head, I looked at the stormy expression in his eyes. "Don't," I said firmly, putting a hand on his face, reveling in the feel of his whiskered jaw under my fingers. "It's not your fault, and I'm safe now. I have a job, and a future because of you."

"Don't be grateful to me," he rasped, using his body weight to pin me down on the couch.

My head hit one of the throw pillows, and I stared up at his furious expression, just inches from mine. "I *am* grateful. How could I not be?" I would very likely be at a homeless shelter somewhere if I hadn't gone to his office begging for a job.

"I don't deserve it. I don't pity you, Eva. I want to fuck you."

I knew that wrapping my arms around his neck was trouble, but I did it anyway. Fire was licking through my body, incinerating its way straight to my core. "Then do it, because the last thing I want is for you to feel sorry for me," I whispered, tired of fighting the rampant attraction between the two of us.

The future didn't matter right now. All I wanted was Trace. I knew I was only here to do a job, but I'd never felt this way about any man before. *Carpe diem!* Never had that expression meant more to me than right now. I wanted to seize the opportunity I had at the moment and not think about tomorrow.

I saw a flash of something resembling satisfaction as he lowered his mouth to mine. Then, I was lost in a world of crazy desire as our tongues and mouths fused in swirling desperation and insane need.

He kissed like a man possessed by a wild fury he couldn't control. He held most of his weight off me, but I would have welcomed it. I wanted to climb inside him, feel our bodies meld and merge in the most elemental way.

I couldn't get enough of him, and maybe one time with Trace wouldn't sate my need, but I didn't think about that. All I could do was...feel.

I panted as he pulled his mouth from mine. I wanted to protest when his weight lifted from my body, wanting to feel him again the moment he moved away.

Licking my lips, I could still taste his embrace as I watched him pull his sweatshirt over his head and dump it on the floor. *Sweet Jesus!* He was perfect. Every flexing muscle looking like it was carved out of stone. His biceps had flexed as he'd relieved himself of his shirt, and his abs were so defined I could see every splendid muscle in his stomach and chest. Smooth skin that I was itching to touch was revealed, and I reached out for him with reflexive longing. I was desperate to see if his skin was as warm as it looked, and I was dying to trace the happy trail of dark hair that disappeared disappointingly into the waistband of his jeans.

"No, Eva," he barked. "If you touch me, I'll lose it."

I *wanted* him to lose it; I *lived* to see him out of control right now.

"I want to touch you."

He ignored my plea and sat me up to take off my sweater. It joined his shirt on the floor. I was giving thanks for Claudette as he removed the pink lacy bra I was wearing, releasing the front catch expertly. I shivered as the cool air hit my hardened nipples, letting him slide the silky undergarment down my arms slowly before discarding it in the growing pile of clothing on the floor.

"Beautiful," he grunted, pushing me back down on the pillow.

I gasped aloud as his hot mouth met my sensitive nipple, sucking it into an ultra-hard peak. "Yes," I whispered, unable to find my full voice.

He closed his fingers around the other tight bud, tugging with just the right pressure to cause a violent spasm in my core.

"Mine," Trace demanding as he lifted his head from my breast.

At that moment, he owned my body, could do anything he wanted to me as long as he satisfied the excruciating ache inside me. "Yes," I agreed.

Slowly, his mouth explored the valley between my breasts, and he tongued his way down my belly. I thrust my hands in his hair roughly, pulling on the strands as my hips lifted, frustrated by the denim between us as I tried to get friction where I needed it most.

His hands tore at the zipper of my jeans, as though he was desperate to get me bared to his hungry eyes.

I lifted my ass as he yanked at my jeans, taking the tiny pink panties down my legs along with my pants.

"Jesus, Eva. You're the most beautiful thing I've ever seen," he said hoarsely, reverently.

I'd never considered myself beautiful. At best, I thought I managed to be mildly attractive. But for one second, one instant, I let myself believe him. Immersing myself in his wild gaze, my breath stopped in my lungs and I was trapped in his intensely beautiful eyes, wishing I'd never get free.

A moan escaped my lips as he spread my legs wide, placing one of my calves over the back of the couch, and the other on the floor. When I was completely open to him, his fingers traced the lips of my pussy.

"You're wet," he rasped.

"Yes." It wasn't like I could deny it. The dewy moisture coating his fingertips was positive proof of how much I needed him.

"I love seeing you like this. You need me. It shows in your eyes."

It was obvious that he needed me, too. His gaze broke from mine, and he looked down to where his fingers were playing.

"I do need you. Fuck me, Trace. Please." I didn't care if I was begging.

His fingers delved through my cleft, and his thumb did a tantalizing circle around my clit.

"I plan on it, sweetheart. But I'm getting addicted to watching your face. I want to see it when you come."

His words set my body off like a human firecracker, electrical waves sizzling from every nerve ending.

"Touch me." I needed him to stop teasing me.

"I can do better than that. I have to taste you."

In the moment it took to process what he was saying, he'd slid down on the couch and lowered his mouth to my core so it could join his teasing fingers.

Unable to stop myself, I screamed his name as his ravenous mouth invaded my pussy, licking, sucking greedily like he never wanted to stop.

"Oh, my God. Oh, my God." I was chanting the same mantra, stunned by the sensation of his mouth feasting on me, his tongue replacing his finger on my clit.

I could hear the sound of my own wetness as he buried his lips, nose and tongue in my core. He tasted, teasing, and then flicked the tiny bundle of nerves that needed his attention, driving my need to the point of insanity.

"Trace. Oh, God. Please. Make me come now." I yanked on his hair, then urged his face to my pussy, letting him know how desperate I really was.

My body tensed unbearably, and I arched my back in agony.

I climaxed on a pitiful, loud, incoherent moan, babbling about how good he made me feel. Waves of ecstasy overwhelmed my senses, and I had no choice but to ride them as Trace lapped at my orgasm like he was trying to savor every drop.

My hands fisted in his hair as I hung on, helpless against the spasms that exploded from my body while Trace wrung every drop of pleasure from me that he could get.

I had achieved release, but I wasn't sated. I watched as he got up and tore off his jeans and boxer briefs, setting his engorged cock free.

I was a bit daunted as I stared at him, but I wanted him inside me worse than I'd ever wanted anything else in my entire life.

Trace fumbled in his wallet and tore out a condom, rolling it on in what I was sure had to be record time.

He came down between my open thighs and kissed me. I sighed into his mouth as our bare skin finally met and slid together, creating a sense of closeness that had my body starting to burn all over again.

My taste was on his lips, and that spurred me on. Right now, he was mine. I loved the fact that my scent was on him everywhere.

Tearing his lips from mine, he started a trail of open-mouthed kisses down my neck.

"Wrap your legs around me," he demanded gruffly.

I obeyed, loving the feel of him trapped between my legs.

The feel of his cock straining for entrance into my body consumed me. I flinched as he pressed harder, trying to breech me.

"Fuck! You're as tight as a virgin, Eva," he said, his voice graveled and desperate.

"Trace, I *am* a virgin." Maybe I should have told him before, but I didn't want him to stop.

"Shit! Why the fuck didn't you tell me?" His expression was fierce, his stare accusing.

"Fuck me. It doesn't matter." I lifted my hips, wanting him buried inside me.

"It sure as hell does matter. Hold on to me. I can't stop."

I was already running my hands over his damp skin, caressing his back. I stopped and grasped his shoulders. "Do it. Please."

Surging forward with a groan, he pushed his way through any barriers that would keep us apart and buried himself inside me. The pain was momentary and slight compared to the fullness and satisfaction I got from knowing he was connected so intimately to me. My muscles balked, and then gave way to his cock, relaxing as they lovingly enfolded him like a glove.

"So tight. So wet. So fucking hot," Trace said huskily. "I'm never going to want to let you go."

I knew he *would* let me go, but I'd worry about that later. Right now, all I wanted to do was experience my first taste of passion with Trace. He was the man I'd been waiting to give my untried body to, the man who could make me ache with desire. "Fuck. Me."

He was clenching his teeth, the muscle in his jaw ticking. I knew he was trying to gain control, and I didn't want him to find it. I tightened my grip with my legs and grinded up against him.

"Hold it, Eva. I can't take you like this. I need to be gentle."

"Screw gentle," I panted. "I need you, Trace. Please."

My words seemed to encourage him, and he pulled himself almost out of my channel before he slammed back in. "I have no fucking control with you," he growled.

He fucked me hard, then harder still, like his life depended on him giving me his cock. I reveled in the soreness, the testing of my muscles as they clenched around him. "Yes. No control. No mercy," I urged, wanting him just as raw and untamed as he could be.

"I can't wait," he said with an urgent groan.

He pistoned in and out of me so hard and fast that my short nails were digging into the smooth skin of his back. I could feel my orgasm rising, bubbling eagerly to release. "Don't wait," I pleaded, needing to watch him come.

He surprised me when his hand slid between our bodies, his fingers searching. I imploded as he put pressure on my clit, forcing me to an explosive climax.

Heat raced through my body, and my channel clamped down on his cock as I rode the waves of ecstasy coursing through my body.

I watched his reaction as he came, his head back, groans of pleasure slipping from his lips as naturally as breathing. "You feel so good, Eva. I never want to fucking leave you."

I never wanted him to go, but I knew I was just living in the moment. There was no other man I'd ever wanted to give my body to, and my first experience had been divine. I hadn't been waiting for anyone in particular, just somebody who made me feel the way Trace did.

We stayed connected, the weight of his body heavy but welcome as we struggled to breathe in the aftermath of a stunning pinnacle I'd never reached before. Stroking the damp skin of his back, I lost track of time. My mind was still reeling when he finally began to leave, placing a quick but passionate kiss on my mouth before he freed himself from my clinging arms.

He slid off me slowly, striding to the bathroom, presumably to lose the used condom.

I laid there watching him, unable to move, unable to think. My mind was as spent as my body.

He'd moved gracefully, without a hint of body shyness. Not that he had any reason to be self-conscious.

Moments later, he was back, and the steady pattern of breathing I'd reestablished became irregular all over again.

He sat and pulled my naked, vulnerable body into his lap. "Tell me. Explain to me why you would let me to take your body when you've never given it to any other man."

"There was no other man I wanted to give it to," I explained breathlessly. "It wasn't like I was saving it for some reason, I just never wanted to be with anyone like that."

He lifted a brow at me. "Nobody in all these years? Where the hell have you been?"

I took in his brooding expression, knowing I was going to have to tell him the truth. I felt vulnerable, stripped bare in a way I'd never experienced before.

"Eva?" His stare was unwavering, waiting.

I felt like he was staring directly into my soul, and God help me, I couldn't lie. "I was in prison. I just finished my parole a year ago. When I was eighteen, I went to a women's correctional facility for three years. I'm sorry. I should have told you. You just fucked a felon."

I hadn't thought about how he'd feel about screwing a convicted criminal. All I had wanted was just a moment to live a dream.

I struggled to get away from him as I saw the shocked look on his face, and for just a second, what I thought was probably revulsion.

I'm a criminal. What did I expect?

Nobody was going to overlook the fact that I'd been a prisoner for most of my adult life. Nobody ever did.

Stumbling to my feet, I turned and ran to my room, not even bothering to pick up my clothes. I locked the door with trembling fingers, turning around and sliding down against it until my bare ass hit the carpet.

Then and only then did I release the anguish that was locked up inside me, sobbing like a small child as I wrapped my arms protectively around my nude upper body and let the torrent begin.

CHAPTER SEVEN

Eva

I was devastated the next morning when the enormity of what I'd said and done the night before really hit me.

I sat up in bed, unrested, and tossed my unruly hair from my face.

"Oh, God," I moaned as I ran a hand down my face.

I told Trace about my past after the most earth shattering moments of my life.

Everything he'd done to me and to my body had felt so damn perfect, every minute surreal. Why had I gone and destroyed it?

"Because there's something about him that won't let me lie," I whispered to myself.

At some point during the night, I'd moved from the floor, undressed and donned a pair of pajamas. The tears had finally dried up, the sobs subsided. I felt worn out, raw and more vulnerable than I ever had in my entire life.

Trace had knocked on the door last night, but I'd stifled my painful cries while he was in the hallway, made myself not utter a sound. He'd finally left, probably assuming I was asleep. Unfortunately, I hadn't slept much, and I'd been very much awake when he'd been hammering on my door. I'd just been too afraid to answer.

"It's Thanksgiving. How am I going to face him?" I flopped onto my back and covered my face with a pillow. I was going to have to face him and live with the fact that he knew my history, and he hadn't accepted it well. There had been anger in his voice last night when he'd come to my bedroom door, and really, could I blame him? I hadn't been honest before he'd laid his hands on me, and he'd unknowingly been intimate with a felon, somebody he shouldn't even know, much less screw.

"Eva!"

I jackknifed into a sitting position as I heard his low baritone outside my door. "I know you're in there. I left last night to give you time, but I'm not leaving again. Answer the door or I break it in." His fist pounded hard on the heavy wood barrier.

Resigned, I scooted out of bed and went to the door, unlocking it and turning around to walk back to the bed and sit.

He entered almost immediately, and I was certain he had been listening for the lock on the door to click. Of course, I was going to unlock it. Number one: there was no way I was going to let him destroy such a beautiful polished wood door. Number two: I couldn't run away from the truth forever. There was no point in putting it off any longer.

I lowered my head and focused on the elegant pattern of the cream-colored carpet on the floor, not wanting to make eye contact with him. My crazy hair hid my face, and I waited.

And waited.

And then, continued to wait.

Every muscle in my body was tense, and I knew he was in the room. Not only had I heard him enter, but I could *feel* him. Trace Walker emitted such a compelling force of energy just by entering a room that he couldn't be ignored.

Just when I was about to give in and look up, I found myself suddenly on my back, pinned by the significant weight of his body.

"What are you doing?" My voice was tremulous as he pinned my hands over my head.

"Don't ever do that again," he demanded in a husky voice.

"Do what?" I couldn't avoid looking at him as he swiped my hair from my face.

"Leave," he growled. "Run away from me. Don't do it again. I fucking hated it."

My heart skittered as I stared at his grim expression. There were dark shadows under his eyes, and I wondered if he'd slept. "You look tired."

"I didn't sleep much. It was hard to fall asleep after I found out I'd screwed a virgin without knowing I was her first. And I damn well knew you were crying."

How had he known? I'd tried not to make a sound. The last thing I wanted was his sympathy.

"I wasn't crying," I told him stubbornly.

"Bullshit!" He frowned and traced what I thought was an invisible line of tears. "Your makeup is smeared."

Shit! Shit! Shit! Damn Claudette and her magic mascara wand.

I was guessing that the telltale sign of my tears was now smeared down my cheeks in a black line of makeup that used to be on my eyelashes. I was going to nix the mascara from now on.

"I did cry, okay. I admit it. I was upset. It's no big deal." I tried to minimize the river of tears I cried the night before, and the release of the sorrow I'd bottled up inside me for years.

As I noticed his expression go from irritation to downright furious, I wondered if he had violent tendencies. He had seemed so in control, so sure of himself. This was a side of Trace that scared me just a little.

"It is a big deal. I hurt you. I'm sorry." His expression was still angry, but his eyes were full of remorse.

"You didn't hurt me. Not really." I didn't struggle in his hold. The weight of his body holding me prisoner was strangely warm and comforting, and his grip on my wrists was only tight enough to keep me from running away…again.

I didn't deserve his guilt over taking my virginity. I'd given it to him willingly because I wanted that experience greedily. Desperately. I wanted someone to cling to for a short time. I wanted to feel like somebody cared. And most of all, I wanted the pleasure he could offer me.

"Then why in the hell did you take off like that?"

I took a deep breath. "I told you that I'm an ex-con. You were disgusted that you'd slept with me. Admit it." I didn't want to hear him say the words, but I *needed* to hear them. My moments of pleasure were over and it was time to face reality.

"I wasn't disgusted with you. I was mad at myself, Eva. I should have known, should have recognized that you were inexperienced. I didn't. I wanted you, and I couldn't think past that. Yes, you surprised me. I was angry, but not at you." He paused for a minute before continuing, "Who set you up? It was your mother, wasn't it?"

I gaped at him. "You think I was innocent?"

He lifted an arrogant brow. "Weren't you?"

"Yes." My chest ached as I realized that he assumed I wasn't guilty of committing the crime that had put me away for most of my adult life.

He shrugged. "I believe you."

Just like that? That easily? He believed I was innocent? "Why?"

He slowly released his grip on my wrists, as though he was reassured I wasn't going anywhere. "Because you've given me no reason to doubt it. You've worked most of your life, and you came to me begging for a job so you could make a living. You were honest when you didn't have to be. I don't think you're capable of whatever crime you supposedly committed."

He helped me sit up, but he kept a supporting hand behind my back.

"You barely know me," I argued, stunned that he didn't appear to have any doubts.

No one had ever believed me, not even a jury of my peers.

"What happened?"

Tears sprang to my eyes again, and I clasped my hands together because I was trembling. Trace was the first person to doubt my guilt, and his exoneration touched my soul. "I don't understand why you believe me."

"Believe it. You don't have to understand why. Just tell me what happened, Eva."

His voice was low and soothing now, and I felt my body finally relax.

One of his large hands reached out and covered my conjoined fingers. "Stop fidgeting. If you did nothing wrong, you have no reason to feel guilty."

It wasn't all guilt that was making me nervous. It was him. Trace made me uneasy, but not in a frightening kind of way. "Nobody has ever believed me. And I don't like to talk about it."

I hated remembering how terrified I was, how I'd been duped by a mother who hadn't given a shit about me. She had known what had happened to me. I'd called her, and she had denied that she'd had anything to do with the crime, but I could tell she'd deliberately left me to take the blame if the theft had been discovered.

"Tell me," Trace said insistently.

I swallowed hard, knowing I owed him an explanation. "My mother didn't work much, but she got a temporary position with a Mrs. Mitchell as an assistant and companion right before she met your father. In fact, she met your dad *because* she worked for the Mitchell family. They were rich. Probably not as rich as your family, but well-to-do." What I really meant was that the Mitchell family probably had *only* millions instead of billions, but they were still incredibly rich. "Mrs. Mitchell introduced your father to my mother during a party."

I turned my head and saw him nod, but he was silent, waiting for me to go on.

"My mother stole some very pricey jewelry from her employer right before her temporary job ended, during an event Mrs. Mitchell was having to celebrate her son's birthday. I came to the festivities to work with my mother - Mrs. Mitchell offered me decent money to come work that night as hired help. I was serving food, and on the cleanup crew. I couldn't turn down the extra income for one night's work. It was a decision I eventually regretted."

"How did you get blamed?" Trace asked curiously.

I shrugged. "My mother left the jewelry in our apartment when she realized your father was going to get serious very quickly. She wasn't going to risk being caught with the goods, so she left them when she went to Texas to be with your father. By the time Mrs. Mitchell raised the alarm and the theft was being investigated, my mother was gone. They found the items in our apartment and I was the only one living there."

"That isn't enough—"

I interrupted before he could say anything more. "Mrs. Mitchell swore my mother would never steal from her. It didn't hurt that your father had already proposed to my mother, and she'd left to live her happily ever after in Texas." I couldn't keep the bitterness out of my voice. "I don't think Mrs. Mitchell wanted to believe that she'd set your dad up with a thief, and she didn't want something like that to go public. There was also video evidence."

"You were caught on video?"

I shook my head. "Not me. It had to be my mother. We both started out wearing the same uniform that afternoon, but she changed shortly after arriving at the mansion because your father was attending the party. She didn't want to be seen as one of the workers. I don't think the Mitchell family ever saw her in the uniform. They weren't around while we were setting up."

"Did she do it on purpose?" Trace's voice was getting irritated.

"Probably."

"So she planned to pin it on you?"

"I really don't think she planned on getting caught. She didn't try to sell the items right away. They were hidden in her room at the apartment. She'd stolen before, and had never gotten caught.

Little stuff. Shoplifting and petty theft. She went big this time, but I think she was too afraid to take the jewelry with her when she went to Texas to be with your dad."

"How in the hell did they mistake her for you in the video?"

"No one remembered seeing her in uniform, and the quality of the video was bad. They could only tell the approximate weight, height and hair color of the person taking the jewelry. That description fit...me. It also fit my mother. Which one do you think they suspected when I had the goods and my estranged mother was marrying a very rich man?"

"Did you confront your mother?"

I nodded. "Only on the phone. She swore she knew nothing about it, and she told me that I needed to pay for my crimes right before she told me that she never wanted to talk to me again and hung up."

My supposed crimes weren't stealing jewelry; I was guilty of just one crime: being born.

"Bitch!" Trace exploded.

I couldn't argue with him. My mother was pure evil. It wasn't something I didn't already know. "The jury unanimously convicted me. I was caught with the goods, I was poor, I was there and wearing the uniform, and I fit the video description of the perp. I was sentenced to four years. I was out in three for good behavior, but I spent time on parole."

"Jesus, Eva. How the hell does a mistake like that happen?" His voice was perplexed, but mostly he sounded angry.

"I was at the wrong place at the wrong time." I'd pretty much come to grips with what had happened in the past. I couldn't change my past or my fate. I could only hope I had a future.

"How did you survive?"

I knew what he meant. He wanted to know how I'd endured being in prison. "It was difficult at first. But I started working in the kitchen at the facility. I kept quiet and stayed out of trouble. I didn't really talk to anyone. I read a lot whenever I could get my hands on books. Time passed." I didn't want to admit that every moment I was in prison seemed like forever, and that staying to myself caused tension with the other women. When I finally left incarceration, I swore I'd never go back. I'd die first.

"And when you got out?" he prompted.

"I got any job I could find. I lied on my job applications, or I stretched the truth. I lost plenty of positions because they found out I was a felon one way or another. When I could, I worked under the table. I did whatever I could to survive."

He gripped my shoulders and turned me toward him. "Why didn't you contact us, Eva? Christ! We would have helped you."

I met his eyes and asked bluntly, "Would you? Would you really? You didn't even know you *had* a stepsister, and the last thing that would have occurred to me is that you'd actually believe me. Nobody else ever has. My mother and your father were dead by the time my trial started. Why would you want to help me? I'm nobody to any of you, and you were dealing with grief and losing your dad. Do you know how hard it was just to get into your office, just to have the chance to talk to you? If you hadn't mistaken me for someone else, I wouldn't have been able to get a conversation with you at all."

He stood and shoved his hands in the pockets of his jeans. "There had to be a way to take care of this, keep you out of prison for a crime you didn't commit."

I smiled as I saw his frustration, his concern over the fact that justice hadn't been done in my case. "You want to think the justice system is infallible. I wanted to think that, too." Unfortunately, I'd learned just how unpredictable it could really be. "My illusions were shattered the minute the verdict was read."

"You were only seventeen, right?"

"I was when the jewelry was stolen, but they found the stolen items in the apartment on the day after my eighteenth birthday. My mother died with your father not long after I was arrested, so I was on my own. I was tried as an adult."

"Fuck!" Trace ran a frustrated hand through his hair, making him look even more gorgeous in a mussed up kind of way. I knew he was trying to make sense out of a situation that was completely unfair.

I knew that look, but he couldn't change what had happened, even if he *was* a Walker.

"It's Thanksgiving. Let me get dressed and I'll cook us an incredible meal. We can forget about what happened for a little while," I suggested, standing up to go take a shower.

Although I was touched that Trace had faith in me, I still didn't have any faith in myself. I didn't want to talk about my past.

Trace grabbed my upper arm as I past and swung me around. "I'll never forget, Eva. I swear I'll make this right."

Looking at his enraged expression, I almost believed him. But after so many years and so many failures, I knew I couldn't outrun my past. "It doesn't matter."

He let go of my arm reluctantly. "The hell it doesn't," he grumbled.

I smiled at him as I shrugged out of his grasp. He couldn't change my past, but I wish I could make him understand how much his belief that I was innocent really meant. Since it was impossible to explain, I simply kept smiling at him weakly and headed for the shower.

CHAPTER EIGHT

Eva

"That was incredible, Eva. It's the best meal I've ever eaten," Trace said earnestly as he sipped a cup of cappuccino in the living room.

I rubbed my belly, wishing I could have eaten more. The Thanksgiving feast had turned out well, and it was the best meal I'd ever eaten. I didn't think it was so much my cooking skills, but Trace's fabulous kitchen. It had every convenience and the fanciest equipment I'd ever used. I was guessing it would be hard to screw up a meal in his kitchen.

"Thanks for letting me cook. Your kitchen is amazing."

He raised a brow as he lifted his mug to his mouth. "You say that like I was doing you a favor instead of vice-versa."

He actually *had* done me a favor. I loved to cook, and his facilities were a cook's dream. "I liked doing it."

I'd been more than a little surprised when he'd pitched in with the cleanup and cleared the table while I loaded the dishwasher. The task had seemed way too domestic for him, but it made me like him even more because he didn't seem to mind helping out, even if it was a job that he usually didn't do.

"I think you should scrap the job at one of the resorts and go to culinary school. It's obviously your passion. You should pursue it as a career," Trace mused, his expression watchful.

"I can't. I need this job, Trace." Cooking was my passion, but I was a realist. I needed to work to survive.

"I can help you get what you should have had, Eva. I want to."

I shook my head. "No. You've helped me enough."

"Nothing I do will ever be enough to undo the past."

"It's not your responsibility to try to make it better," I told him calmly.

"I'm your stepbrother," he argued.

A chuckle escaped my lips. If he was playing the "you're my family" card, I knew he was desperate. He usually chose not to acknowledge that he was related to me by marriage.

Probably because he'd just screwed me the night before.

"What? I am your family," he said stubbornly.

"We have no connection, Trace, and you know it. You don't owe me anything, and even if you did, you've done me a huge favor by giving me work."

The fact that my mother married his father meant absolutely nothing. He hadn't even known my mother, so it wasn't like he could claim a connection through her.

"I'm not offering because of our connection. I want to do it because you have a real talent, Eva. You should be able to do what you want to do."

"Did you?" I asked hesitantly. Trace had been young when his father had died, way too young to take on the responsibilities of the world the way he did now.

He shrugged. "Mostly. I always knew I'd take Dad's place someday. Sebastian wasn't interested in business, and Dane's an amazing artist. I don't think either one of them had any desire to be Dad's successor."

"You never wanted something different?"

"I wanted things to work out differently. I wanted Dad with me a hell of a lot longer than he stayed alive. And I wanted Dane to never have experienced the pain he did. I wanted some time to get my MBA and work a little more on perfecting my mixed martial arts skills. I competed in college a little, but I wanted...more."

"You do MMA?" Okay, I was surprised, but maybe I shouldn't have been. The guy moved lightning fast, and it was evident that he worked out.

"Only as a hobby."

"Did you finish your master's degree?"

"Of course. It took me a while because I was filling Dad's role in the company, but I finished."

Of course you did!

Was there anything Trace Walker couldn't do?

Obviously, the one thing he couldn't accomplish was managing his brothers' lives.

"So your brothers aren't part of the company now?" I was curious.

"No. It's just me. I bought them out because they didn't want the same things. Both of them are incredibly wealthy men, but they aren't in the Walker conglomerate anymore. It's not what they wanted."

"What do they want?" *What do you want?*

"I think they're pretty much doing what they want," Trace said sarcastically. "Sebastian does as little as possible when it involves work, and Dane lives outside of society on a private island. His work is in demand, but he doesn't make personal appearances."

"Are his injuries that bad?" I wondered what had made Dane separate himself completely.

"I don't know. He's my brother. I've never looked at him as anything except my family. I guess I don't notice any of his scars anymore."

"You're worried," I observed.

"Yes." Trace sounded reluctant to admit his concern.

"You're not responsible for their current situations, any more than you're guilty of the plane crashing." Trace was shouldering the burden of his siblings' wellbeing, and he needed to let go. His brothers were adults, and needed to find their own ways.

"I'm their older brother," he argued gruffly.

"Exactly. You're not their father." He needed to understand that even though he had taken on his father's role in the company, his brothers were never going to see him as anything other than their oldest sibling. In fact, they might end up resenting him for trying to fix them.

I could easily see all of these issues because I was an outsider. I know that, for Trace, letting go was a struggle. He tried to act like he didn't care, but he cared very much. *Maybe too much.* Easy for me to say, I guess, considering I had nobody. But my heart ached for the suffering this family had been through. And judging by what little Trace had shared, the family was still broken.

We were silent for a few minutes, Trace looking like he was lost in thought. I finished my coffee and sat the mug carefully on the end table next to my chair. He finished his moments later, and placed his used cup on the coffee table in front of him.

"Britney is definitely my fault," he confessed with a stoic expression. "She went after Dane specifically because I dumped her."

"She's a poisonous snake," I grumbled. "And it's not your fault she sought Dane out. That's all on her."

It made my stomach roll to think that a woman could prey on a man who was as vulnerable as Dane.

"You make it sound like nothing is my fault." There was humor in Trace's voice.

"I'm sure you're guilty of many things, but not your brothers' problems. Both of them are wealthy, grown men who can choose what they want to do."

"What am I guilty of then?" His tone was teasing.

You're guilty of breaking my heart over a family that I've never even met. You're guilty of making me care whether you're all put together again, even though I've always hated the Walker name in the past. You're guilty of doing things to me, making me feel emotions I've never had before. And it's starting to mess with my head.

I took a deep breath. "I think you're incredibly bossy, and you hate it when things don't go exactly the way you want. I think your control is so important to you because if you ever lost it, it would make you less like your father. In your eyes, that would be almost unforgivable. I think you care about your brothers' wellbeing more than you want to admit. And I think you're a wonderfully generous man, but that's a side of you that you don't let anyone see."

"I think you're crazy." Trace was frowning now.

I raised a brow, mimicking his expression when he was annoyed. "You think so?"

He nodded curtly. "I'm an asshole because I have to be. Business gets nasty."

"You're distant because you *have* to be. Do you think I don't understand that?" I'd spent years being distant, having only books as friends while I stared at the same concrete walls and bars every single day. I got it. Obviously, he didn't. For him, the distance wasn't deliberate. It was the way he lived his life to protect himself.

"Maybe you do understand," he said grudgingly. Trace stood and held out his hand. "Come with me."

I knew that he was changing the subject because he wasn't comfortable with talking about himself, but I let him off the hook. Hell, sometimes there were things I didn't want to deal with either. I let him tug me to my feet and I followed in his wake as he made his way to his home office.

"You asked about the cell phone. I had some things delivered for you, things I knew you would need."

And he thinks he's an asshole? The breath *whooshed* from my lungs as he arrived at his destination and pointed toward a pile of goods that took up half of the floor space in his office. "What did you do?" I asked breathlessly.

He'd already provided me a new wardrobe to play my part. Did I really need all this?

"Your new phone." He unplugged the latest model iPhone from the charger and handed it to me. "I think it has everything you'll need installed."

I took the cell from him automatically, still gaping at the ton of things he thought it was necessary for me to have.

A new laptop computer.

A digital camera.

A Kindle e-reader?

I reached out and touched the marvelous device that was capable of bringing me something I dearly loved: unlimited books.

"I thought you'd like it. I opened an account for you, and loaded it with funds from a gift card. You can get as many books as you want."

Oh. My. God. He'd went so far overboard on what I really needed, but it touched me that he'd been listening to me when I told him I loved to read. "Trace, I don't need all of these things. They aren't necessities."

"Some women would argue about that," he answered drily.

"I wouldn't. I know exactly what I need to survive." I picked up another box. "What's this?"

He shrugged. "Jewelry. If we're engaged, I've obviously given you stuff. Gifts."

I dropped the box instantly, recoiling from the thought of jewelry. "I don't want it."

"Don't, Eva. I know how you feel about the past, but these are gifts."

"Not jewelry." I shook my head and backed away from the plethora of electronics, jewelry and gifts.

"Yes. If we're together, I'd make you accept every damn thing I wanted to give you." He turned and strode to his desk and brought back a small box that didn't look new. He held it out to me. "Your engagement ring."

I swallowed hard and tried to breathe. I couldn't wear expensive jewelry. "I can't." My voice was cracking with emotion, and tears sprung to my eyes.

Trace opened the black velvet box and took the ring out. "Yes, you can." He took my hand and slowly worked the ring onto my finger. "It's necessary."

I held out my hand when he was finished, noticing that I was actually shaking. The ring was stunning. Princess cut and probably several carats, it sparkled with a fire that was nearly blinding. "It's beautiful, but it's enormous. What if I lose it?"

Shit, I'd be terrified every single day with this rock on my finger.

"It belonged to my mom, so I'd prefer you didn't take it off," he answered huskily.

I gaped up at him. "Oh, my God. Can't we pick something else?" The giant diamond had sentimental value to him, and I didn't want to be responsible for losing something that belonged to his mother.

He grinned at me. "No. I'm the oldest son. My fiancée would be expected to wear it, unless you hate it."

"I don't hate it," I rushed to assure him. "It's amazing." I was telling the truth. The ring was magnificent, but I was terrified to have it on my finger. "But it means something to you, and I don't want anything to happen to it."

"Nothing will happen. And it looks good on your finger. It fits almost perfectly."

Yes, it did. His mother must have had almost the same ring size. "That's not the point."

"You need to wear the ring, and I hope you'll wear the other stuff I bought for you. That jewelry is all yours. I bought it."

I tried taking deep breaths to control my panic. I couldn't believe he was trusting a woman who had done time for stealing expensive jewelry with a priceless heirloom, and a ton of other expensive gems. What was he thinking? Yeah, he'd said he trusted me, but I hadn't realized quite how much...until now.

Trace really does believe I could never steal anything.

He sat down in a brown leather chair near the pile of gifts, then grasped my hand and yanked me down onto his lap. I struggled for balance, but finally righted myself with Trace's protective grip on my waist, and my arms wrapped around his neck.

I looked down at him from my perch on his thighs, sighing as I saw the hungry look on his face. "I'm not sure I can do this."

"Are you backing out of our deal?" he growled, his grip tightening around me.

I shook my head. "No. But all of this is mind-blowing, Trace. And for obvious reasons, I hate jewelry."

"This is different, Eva. And I love seeing my mother's ring on your finger."

"Why?" I asked curiously.

"Because it means that for now, you belong to me."

I didn't have time to babble a response before he snaked a hand around the back of my neck and pulled my lips down none-too-gently to capture my mouth.

CHAPTER NINE

Trace

I knew from the moment I saw my mother's ring on her finger that I was screwed. Every well-meant intention I'd had to keep my hands off Eva had completely flown from my mind.

Yeah, I knew I shouldn't touch her again. She'd been a virgin, and I felt bad enough for the way I'd taken her, but that didn't matter anymore.

She's. Fucking. Mine.

My hand moved to her silky hair and I fisted it to try to regain control as I claimed her mouth just as thoroughly as possible, my dick demanding to be inside her.

My heart slammed hard and fast against the wall of my chest as she moaned against my lips, music to my ears.

I wanted to fuck her again, this time slow and gentle like I should have done last time. Problem was, I wasn't sure I could stay in control with Eva. I wanted to own her: heart, body and soul. I wanted to be so deep inside her and make her feel so good that she'd never want another man.

In a way, I'd actually been screwed since I'd realized she was a virgin. Primitive emotions had swamped me then, grappling with my common sense. All I could think about was that I didn't ever want her to have any other man...except me. Hell, I probably would have felt the same way if she hadn't been untouched. I was just that obsessed with her.

I broke off the kiss and rasped against the soft skin of her neck, "I won't do this again. I can't fuck you again." Jesus, I hated it when the higher, more noble emotions got in the way of me getting what I wanted. I'd much prefer to give into the barbarian and take what I wanted.

"Why?"

The disappointment in her voice damn near broke me. "It's not fair to you. I was a greedy bastard, and I never even thought to ask if you were a virgin. It should have been different for you."

It should have happened with a man you loved, a guy who could make you feel special.

After everything she'd been through, she deserved that and more.

"It *did* happen just the way I wanted it. No one has ever made me feel the way you do, Trace. Please don't regret it," she pleaded.

That was the problem. I actually *didn't* regret it. I relished the fact that I was the only damn man to be inside her, and it made me possessive. I didn't like feeling that way, but I couldn't seem to stop myself when it came to Eva. "I don't," I admitted reluctantly. "And it's going to be hell when we have to sleep in the same bed."

"Why would we do that?" she asked in a distracted voice, a tone that made me realize she was sexually frustrated. Immediately, I wanted to satisfy her need.

"You're my fiancée. Don't you think it would be a little strange if we don't sleep together?" I knew that would be a big red flag for my brothers.

"I suppose," she answered wistfully.

"We'll manage," I said abruptly, moving her slowly off my lap before I could act on the impulses bombarding me, the instinct to claim her again.

She wriggled as she went to stand, and I had to hold back a groan as her luscious ass moved around on my swollen cock. Christ! It took everything I had not to strip her naked and have her ride me into oblivion right here in the chair.

Watching her as she fidgeted, messing nervously with her hair and then smoothing imaginary wrinkles from her jeans and sweater, I felt the sudden need to protect her. Eva had come to enough harm in her short life, and she didn't need further pain from me.

"Let's take some of this stuff to your room," I suggested in a hoarse voice as I stood. I needed a distraction or I was going to lose it.

"It's too much, Trace. I realize that I have to wear the ring, but the other stuff..." she threw her hands up in the air.

I grinned because I had to. What woman didn't want to accept gifts?

Only Eva.

And she wondered why I trusted her? Granted, it was more gut instinct than proof, but I would stake my life on the fact that she wasn't guilty of her supposed crimes. My gut had never steered me wrong. Unfortunately, I couldn't take away the pain she'd suffered in the past. But I was going to give her a better future, even if I had to fight her to do it.

I'd win.

I always did.

"You're taking it or you're fired." I tried to make my tone firm.

She was adorable when she put her hands on her hips, and she lifted her chin stubbornly. "You won't fire me."

Nope. I wouldn't. It would kill me not to know where she was and how she was doing. But I didn't say that. "Don't tempt me," I grumbled.

"I'd like to go shopping tomorrow. I'd like to buy something for your brothers for Christmas. Can I borrow one of your fancy cars?"

I didn't give a damn if she took any one she wanted, and it didn't escape my notice that she hadn't agreed to accept my gifts, but she would. I was fine with her doing whatever made her happy. Except it meant that I'd be alone in the house, and the idea didn't appeal to me at all. I'd planned to go to the office early in the mornings, and then get back home in the afternoons. The ball had already been set into motion to investigate exactly why Eva had been in jail, and to view the supposed evidence. I was going to do whatever it took to right the wrongs that had been done to her as soon as possible.

"I'll go with you," I answered, resigned. "I haven't bought things for my brothers either."

Fuck! I hated shopping. I usually left all Christmas gifts to my employees.

"Where is your tree?" Eva looked at me hopefully.

"My employees haven't put it up yet." But they would. Because my family was coming, I'd eventually have a Christmas tree. It was another one of those things that just appeared without me thinking about it.

Her horrified expression was almost amusing. "You can't let your employees put up your tree. It should be a tradition," she answered emphatically.

"I'm alone. What does it matter?" Most years I didn't even bother with a tree at home.

"It matters. I always had some kind of tree, even if I had to find one that was discarded and put it up with homemade decorations."

My gut rolled just at the thought of Eva underage and so damn alone, hungry and afraid. If her mother wasn't already dead, I'd be tempted to kill the bitch myself. "The tree will get put up eventually."

"Or we could pick our own and put it up ourselves."

Her tone was so damn hopeful that I was completely destroyed. I'd give her everything she ever needed and more. "If you wish," I agreed.

Nothing had ever felt better than having Eva hurl herself at me and put her arms around my neck, pressing her entire cuddly body against mine. My arms wrapped around her automatically to steady her after her precarious dive into my harder form.

"Thank you, Trace," she said tearfully. "It would be amazing to put a tree in this house. It will look incredible. I haven't truly been able to decorate a normal tree for such a long time, since Dad died."

Such a small thing, with such a big response. It was almost humbling how easily I could make her happy. It was also distressing. If a simple Christmas tree could make her happy, it told the story of how difficult her life had really been.

"We'll get a really big tree," I grumbled, rubbing a hand on her back. I wasn't sure if I was consoling her or trying to sooth my anger.

"Everything worthwhile doesn't have to be big." She pulled back slightly and smiled.

Yeah, I'm an asshole, but I couldn't resist. I grinned at her. "Sometimes it's much more enjoyable if it's big enough."

She understood immediately, just like I knew she would. Giving my arm a smack, she answered cheekily as she rolled her eyes, "Pervert. Is everything all about getting laid with you?"

Hell, yes. It had been since I met her. I've never met a woman who could make me run around hard all the fucking time. Yep… pretty much all I could think about was being inside her again. "Pretty much."

Eva's delighted laughter filled the room, and I felt my heart pounding erratically against the wall of my chest. Jesus! There was nothing better than hearing her sound young and carefree. I wished I could make everything like that for her all the time. She was young, but she'd never had much to smile about. Still, she could laugh at little things, stuff I didn't even think about.

"Do you get the newspaper?" Laughter was still there in her voice.

I shrugged. "I probably do." It appeared when I wanted it, so I assumed I did get the paper.

"You don't know?"

"No. It's usually on the table in the morning. So I guess it gets delivered. Why do you want it?"

She pulled slowly away from me, and my dick was screaming in protest.

"Black Friday deals. I wanted to look at the fliers."

"Who shops for Black Friday?" It wasn't like I didn't know that there were massive sales the day after Thanksgiving. But a sale was never worth getting trampled over just to get merchandise. Hell, I didn't even let my employees shop for me until the madness had calmed down.

"Me," she answered quietly. "I've never had my own money before. I want to get a good deal on gifts."

She sounded so serious that I didn't dare laugh at her. "People get killed getting those deals." I wasn't thrilled about the thought of her getting stampeded, and I was suddenly damn happy I was going with her.

"People get killed doing almost anything," she scoffed. "It might be a little crazy, but I think it would be fun to shop tomorrow during all the big sales."

Fun? Seriously?

Shit! If it meant she would be smiling and laughing, I was screwed. I'd be in the stores on the craziest day imaginable to actually *shop* just to see her happy. "Fine. But no door buster sales."

She covered her smile with her hand, but I knew she was laughing at me anyway. The little witch. Did she know she had me doing things I wouldn't normally do, just to see her acting like any other woman her age? Well, maybe not women I personally knew, but probably the majority of normal women in their twenties. Honestly, I didn't think she had any idea how much I wanted to make things better for her. Eva wasn't the type to manipulate or take advantage. She was simply joyful about everyday things she'd never had.

"Okay. Nothing at four a.m. or earlier," she agreed. "How about six or seven o'clock sales?"

I looked at her pleading expression, and I was done. Her dark eyes were too damn expressive, too damn enthusiastic. I fell into her mesmerizing gaze so easily it was pretty scary. "Eight o'clock."

I'd compromise and hope most of the craziness had ended during the wee hours of the morning.

Nobody would ever miss me in the office since the entire company had the day off. I would have been the only one who was actually in the office tomorrow, and it probably would have been a productive day. But it suddenly didn't matter.

"Okay," she agreed hastily. "Can I use the computer? I can look at the sales online."

"Of course. It's your computer." She was taking it whether she wanted it or not.

"I meant your desktop."

"Use yours." I wanted her to get used to having her own stuff.

"I don't have one."

I picked up the new laptop on the floor and handed it to her. "Let's go find the sales." Those words were foreign to me even as they rolled off my tongue. I'd never looked at sale items in my entire life.

"Trace, I can't accept all this—"

"Of course you can," I insisted, getting irritated because she wouldn't take what I'd willingly given to her.

"I hurt your feelings," she observed quietly. "Please understand how I feel. I'm not used to this."

"Get used to it," I told her in an ornery voice that I reserved for stubborn people, which fit Eva perfectly.

Making sure she had a good grip on the computer, I gave free reign to my caveman instincts and picked her up bodily and carried her out of the room before she could launch another protest.

I was going to win.

I always do.

CHAPTER TEN

Eva

The following few weeks that I spent alone with Trace were some of the best days of my life. The Christmas tree was beautiful. Once I'd convinced him to get a real tree, we'd had a wonderful evening decorating...after Trace had figured out how to put on the lights. That particular process had been filled with plenty of curses that made me laugh, watching him struggle with strings of lights. I was still amazed that he'd never decorated a tree himself, even as a child.

I got unlimited access to his kitchen, and his staff was more than willing to fetch anything I wanted from the grocery store. I'd borrowed his car a few times to go out myself, and he'd never blinked an eye at giving over the keys to one of his expensive vehicles. I just wished he'd had a Chevy or Ford in his collection, something that didn't make me a nervous wreck to drive. Unfortunately, I'd been stuck driving a Ferrari. Trace had insisted that it was the least expensive of the lot, but I was too stressed to ask exactly what it was worth. I was pretty sure I didn't want to know.

A few days before Dane's arrival with the bitchy Britney, I sat in the living room just staring at the enormous tree we'd put together. Trace was on the couch devouring the frosted Christmas sugar cookies I'd made earlier in the day, and judging by the ecstatic grunts he made between bites, he liked them.

I'd made us both a coffee to go with the cookies, well aware that the happiness I'd found in the last few weeks was about to come to an end. Once his brothers arrived, the acting part of this job was going to begin. Strangely, it wasn't going to be hard to pretend I cared about Trace. Honestly, I was getting so addicted to him that it was pathetic. Because I was so attracted to him in some strange and mysterious ways, the sexual tension was always there, but I also just...liked him. I loved being with him. He made me feel important, like I was somehow special.

"Jesus, Eva. Don't ever leave me. These are the best cookies I've ever had," he said as he came up for air from his cookie orgy.

I smiled at him over the mug of coffee I was holding, from my position on the other end of the couch. "You said that about the fudge and the other cookies, too." God, I loved that about him. I loved the way he didn't think twice about complimenting me for something he enjoyed. Or how good I looked, no matter how sloppily I was dressed. There wasn't a single day that I didn't get encouragement from Trace for one reason or another, and I wasn't used to being praised. It warmed me like nothing else possibly could.

He nodded. "They were amazing, too."

I rolled my eyes at him, but I secretly loved the flattery. "So tell me about Dane. He'll be here Monday." It was Friday night, and I still knew so little about his family. Sebastian would arrive next week as well, and I felt like I didn't have the details a fiancée would have on Trace's family.

Trace and I talked about little things, and he'd shared stories about him and his two brothers from his childhood. They'd sounded like happy times, but I was interested to know what had happened since then.

"He'd never leave his Island if he could get away with it. I had to convince him that he needed to come here for Christmas."

Trace's voice was stoic, but there was a sad inflection in his tone that he couldn't hide.

"You said you don't notice his scars. But how would they look to an outsider?" I wasn't worried about Dane's scars. I'd seen some pretty beaten up people, and I doubted much could shock me. But I wanted to know if he'd been shunned or ridiculed.

"I suppose they'd be unpleasant," Trace said grudgingly. "He's had more surgeries than I can count, but they're still noticeable. He was burned over a large percentage of his body, and he broke a lot of facial bones. He's healed, but the scars are still there."

"Does he talk about it?"

He shook his head. "Never."

Okay. Note to self: don't mention the accident or Dane's scars. "I'll make sure the subject doesn't come up. What does he like to talk about?"

"Dane's not much of a talker, but he's always ready to discuss any kind of art."

"I'm not exactly versed in the world of art," I said thoughtfully.

"It doesn't matter. It's not like he can't make polite conversation. He grew up in the world of the rich and superficial."

Trace was grinning at me, and I smiled back at him. "I guess I just want to find common ground with your brothers. I want them to like me."

"You don't have to be anything except yourself and they'll like you," Trace muttered, unconcerned.

"You mean a convicted felon who knows nothing about polite conversation with the super-rich?"

I was, after all, an imposter. Trace and I had agreed on our story, that we had met at a party that I was helping to cater. The rest was a little vague.

"You're not a convicted felon," he growled, sitting his coffee and empty plate on the coffee table to glare at me.

"Pull a background check," I replied morosely.

"Okay," he agreed readily. "I'll let you do it."

I gaped at him, confused, but I jumped up and followed him into his office.

He sat me down in his enormous chair, messing with the computer in front of me, caging me between his arms that were extended to the keyboard.

God, he smelled good. I closed my eyes and inhaled, knowing I'd never forget his masculine essence. I could catch a whiff of light sandalwood, but the rest was all uniquely his scent, and my mouth watered to drink him in completely.

"Eva?"

My eyes popped open and I turned to look at him. "I'm sorry. My mind...wandered."

"Put in your information. This is our background check pre-screening for job applicants. It picks up public records. We do a more thorough check if this comes out clean. If you're a felon, we'd know."

Squinting at the tiny print on the screen, I quickly filled in the information requested.

"Run it," he insisted.

I pushed the button to start the check, my heart beating so fast that I couldn't breathe. I knew what it was going to show, and I hated seeing it in writing. "You know it's going to come up."

He was silent, his focus on the screen. As soon as the report came back, he reached past me and pressed the button to print. He grabbed the report from his printer and quickly scanned it, then dropped it in front of me. "It's clean," he announced smugly.

My sweaty palm gripped the papers, and I rifled through the few pages that had printed. My past addresses were listed, and my employment from high school.

It's not here.

"The report isn't extensive enough," I reasoned.

"Bullshit. It picks up any recorded criminal records. Yours is clean."

93

I shook my head, mystified as to why it wasn't showing. "That's not possible."

"It isn't there because it's been deleted."

I turned my head to gape at him. "How?"

"After the video was cleaned up, it was evident that it was your mother and not you. It was a shitty video that proved nothing, but I have the technology to make it clearer. I also had a talk with Mrs. Mitchell, and a discussion with the prosecution. I knew you didn't want to go through a lengthy process, so it was just... deleted from your record."

Deleted? How could years of my adult life just go away? "You did it." I was doubtful that the prosecution would just purge it from my records.

"Does it matter how it happened? It's gone."

No, it really *didn't* matter. Whether Trace had accomplished the miracle on his own, or whether he'd had assistance, he freed me from the past.

"No. No, it doesn't matter."

"It will never take away what you had to endure, Eva. But it's only fair that you don't have to live with the crime on your record."

"I'm free," I mumbled in wonder. "I don't have to worry about losing a job again over my criminal history."

"No. I promise you the record will never show anywhere again."

Tears formed and started pouring down my cheeks. How did a person thank somebody for doing something like this? "I don't know what to say. I don't know how to thank you."

"You can start by never mentioning the subject again, and not putting yourself down because you have a record. You don't. Not anymore."

Still looking at him and the fierce green light in his eyes, I started to sob. It wasn't delicate or attractive. The tortured sounds escaping my mouth was a release of the pain that had been trapped inside me for a very long time. It was almost painful to let that anguish out of confinement.

Trace didn't say a word. He simply lifted me out of the chair and strode back to the living room, allowing me to let go of the agony of the past.

All of my fear.

All of the excruciating hurt.

My sense of betrayal.

My terror of finding myself in prison.

My profound sense of being alone.

As I clung to him, those things truly became part of my past, a past that had no place interfering with my future.

"I can't believe you did this for me," I wailed against his shoulder.

"Believe it. I would do it over and over again if I had to." His arms tightened as he rocked his body, making me sway along with him.

"Thank you. I wouldn't have been able to do this without you," I choked out.

"I'll always be here for you, Eva. You aren't alone anymore," he answered hoarsely.

What Trace didn't know was that he'd never be alone either. He'd stolen a piece of my heart and soul, and I knew right then and there that I'd never get those back again.

I had a hard time sleeping that night. I'd gotten out of bed and wandered to the kitchen, snatching a few cookies and a glass of milk. I stood in the dimly-lit kitchen, scarfing cookies at the counter, my unblemished past still seeming too surreal to take in.

I missed the feel of Trace's arms around me, his strong, hard body sheltering me. He'd held me for what seemed like hours before we finally said goodnight, and now I was lonely.

I know I'm going to have to get used to being alone again shortly. Rationally, I understood that, but it couldn't diminish the longing of my body and mind right now.

I swallowed the last of my cookie and washed it down with milk before placing the cup in the dishwasher.

I picked up my phone that had finished charging on the counter, searching for Isa's number. I'd finally told her the truth during a long telephone conversation earlier in the week. I'd avoided her because I was ashamed of the fact that we'd arranged for me to go to culinary school, but I'd ended up in prison instead. My shame had kept me from calling her earlier, but Trace had urged me to get in touch with her. Since he'd wiped away my record and proved my innocence, my sense of embarrassment had finally fled.

Isa had comforted me, let me talk about my insecurities. She'd also prompted me to go on with my plans for school since Trace had given me enough money to get started. I didn't know exactly what I was going to do, but Isa had offered to be there to help me with anything I needed, and we'd planned to get together for lunch after the holidays.

She knew everything, even that I had feelings for Trace. I hadn't admitted that I'd slept with him, but she'd guessed the truth.

Are you awake? I sent her the short text. It was getting late, but I figured if she was asleep, she wouldn't reply.

My phone rang seconds later.

"Is everything okay?" Isa asked anxiously.

"It's fine. I didn't mean to bother you."

"You're not. I'm waiting up for Robert. He had an emergency at work."

My heart swelled. Isa sounded so incredibly happy. "You love him."

"With all of my heart," Isa admitted happily. "How's Trace?"

"He's good. In bed. I couldn't sleep."

We made small talk for a while, catching up on what we had done in the last week.

"You sound like you're crazy about Trace," Isa observed.

"I think I am."

"Then don't let him go, Eva," she said sternly.

"I have to, Isa. We have no future, and he doesn't want me forever."

She sighed into the phone. "In some cases, you have to take one day at a time. I didn't think Robert and I had a future either. But one day we realized that we didn't want to be apart. It didn't happen overnight. Sometimes you need to be open to letting things grow naturally."

With Trace, I wasn't sure things hadn't already grown into a jungle for me. "He's a billionaire, and I'm a woman who has been to prison. What kind of crazy combination is that?"

"Robert's rich, and I'm a girl from the wrong side of the tracks," Isa reminded me.

"But you bettered yourself—"

"Just as *you* will. Be patient, Eva. Give yourself a break. Trace would be lucky to have you. There aren't many women who aren't going to care only about his money."

"His money doesn't matter," I admitted. "It's just...*him.*"

"Then go after what you want. Lord knows you're stubborn enough. You lived through your childhood and a bad start as an adult. You deserve some happy time."

We talked a little longer, then solidified our plans to meet up after the holidays. After we hung up, I thought about the conversation, wondering if I needed to be bold and just live in the moment for a change.

Go. Find him. Take whatever pleasure you can get for right now. Enjoy the fantasy, because reality will crash down on you all too soon.

I wasn't a live-for-today kind of woman. But I'd planned my future once, and all of those dreams had never happened. Maybe I should learn how to live in the moment, seize what I wanted.

Right now, what I needed was Trace.

I wondered if he still wanted me, but I was pretty certain our attraction was mutually hot. The tension arched between us every time we were together, and it was getting to both of us. My body clamored for satisfaction, and I wouldn't be satiated without him.

Quietly, I moved through the house, finding my way to his room in the near-darkness. There were a few nighttime lights on, but most of the house was dark.

"I don't know if I can do this," I whispered to myself as I arrived at Trace's bedroom door.

Oh yes, I *could* do it. I *wanted* to do it. I needed to be close to Trace right now, and if I had to expose my need to him to get my wish, I didn't give a damn.

I turned the handle and pushed open the door, relieved to find it open. His shutters weren't closed, and the moonlight illuminated his sleeping form as I walked closer to the bed.

God, he was beautiful. On his back, the sheet and comforter down to his waist, my core clenched ferociously as I got a glimpse of Trace's sculpted chest. He looked more relaxed in sleep, but just as hot as he ever did. A lock of hair had fallen over his forehead, and I had to clench my fist to keep from reaching to smooth it back into place. He looked like a perfectly sculpted statue without a single blemish, and my heart nearly rocketed out of my chest.

I looked away from him, unable to hide my desire or my carnal thoughts. I wanted Trace Walker in a confusing and very elemental way. There was no denying it. I wanted desperately to touch him, let him claim me the same way he had a few weeks ago.

Before I had a chance to think, I slid into the bed beside him. "Eva?"

I had to answer. "Yes."

"Why are you here? Is something wrong?" His voice was low, masculine, and husky with sleep, but his concern was immediately present.

"We have to sleep together eventually. I just thought..." Oh hell, I didn't know what I was thinking.

My body was imprisoned quickly as he said, "I can't have you in my bed and not fuck you, Eva. It's not possible."

"I can't be here and not want you to," I admitted in a tremulous voice.

Trace had rolled on top of me, holding me captive with his body weight. I couldn't see his eyes, but I could make out his tortured expression.

"I have no business being with you, Eva. But since you've come here, I doubt I can send you away. I want you too damn much."

It sounded like a threat, but I took it as I wanted to. He wanted me, and that's all I cared about. "I want to be with you, Trace. I wouldn't be here if I didn't."

"I don't suppose you're on birth control."

"Actually, I am. I have been since I was sixteen." The last thing I needed was an unwanted pregnancy, and even though I was comfortable there, I *had* lived in a rough neighborhood. I'd been put on the pill as much for protection against the unthinkable as I did it to help with my irregular periods.

"Christ! I hope you trust me, that you know I wouldn't take you without a condom unless you believe I've been checked and I'm clean."

"I believe you," I replied breathlessly. I trusted him utterly and completely.

"Good. Because I don't have condoms. I figured if I got rid of them all, I wouldn't be tempted to fuck you again. But now you're out of luck," he warned.

I smiled into the darkness and wrapped my arms around his neck, my fingers stroking his neck. "Maybe I wanted to seal my own doom," I teased.

"You succeeded then." He swooped down and covered my mouth with his.

CHAPTER ELEVEN

Eva

I wallowed in the scent and feel of Trace, refusing to feel guilty because I was seizing what I wanted. I knew I wouldn't regret being with him. In fact, I wanted to or I wouldn't be here. I'd been a virgin for way too long, and I was eager to find the high only Trace could give me.

Our tongues dueled and entwined, and I could feel the rapid rise and fall of his chest above me as he rested his body on mine. I hated the simple cotton nightgown that separated our bodies, and I wanted it gone. My breasts were hard and sensitive, and all I wanted was to feel Trace skin-to-skin.

His wild mouth consumed me, and I gave back exactly what he was giving me: passion, desperation, the incredible need to join our bodies together to sooth the aching need in my body and soul.

Finally, he released my lips and trailed hot, open-mouthed kisses down the sensitive skin of my neck.

I pushed my hips up, straining as I moaned, "I need you, Trace. Fuck me."

"Slower this time, sweetheart," he demanded.

"Fast. Hard. And as deeply as you can," I countered, knowing what my body had to have.

"No. I didn't get to savor you before. But I'm going to do it this time if it kills me," he answered assertively against my skin.

I didn't want to be savored. I wanted to be fucked. Letting my hand slide down his back, I realized he was completely nude. The temptation to touch him made me try to force a hand between our bodies. "I need to touch you."

"Baby, you can't," he commanded. "I'd never last. Relax, Eva. Let me show you how good it can be."

I sighed and moved my wayward hand up his back. "I don't feel relaxed. I feel desperate," I whimpered.

"I know. But I'll take care of that."

"When?" My voice was demanding.

I heard him chuckle as he pulled the nightgown over my head, leaving me completely exposed because I wasn't wearing panties. "Soon, my sweet Eva." He tossed the garment he'd removed to the floor.

He tongued my skin, tasting as he made his way down my body. When he palmed one of my breasts, the breath left my body.

I moaned as his thumb caressed the swollen nipple at the same time his mouth descended on the other one. My body pulsed, and his touch was incinerating me. I wasn't sure I was going to live through his savoring.

"Please, Trace. I need you."

"I need you, too, baby. But just let me satisfy you."

He moved down more, and his tongue leisurely flicked into my navel, and then left a trail of flames down my lower belly.

My fingers gripped a handful of the bottom sheet as his hot breath wafted over my pussy.

"God. Yes." I could barely get the words out.

He parted my legs wider, placing them far apart. He grabbed a pillow and placed it beneath my ass, bringing his face level with the part of me that needed his attention the most.

Then, without hesitation, he devoured me. His tongue darted through my folds and into my saturated core, lapping at my juices as though he couldn't get enough.

"Trace. Oh my God. Please." I needed release, and I gripped the sheets tighter, needing to hang onto something to keep myself grounded.

His tongue circled the pulsating bundle of nerves several times teasingly before he took my engorged clit between his teeth and flicked it with his tongue over and over again.

I screamed as he used his other hand, delving into my channel with one finger, and then he added another. The stretching sensation burned, but it wasn't painful. Somehow, he found that sensitive spot inside me and caressed my g-spot with every fucking stroke of his fingers.

My back arched, my body on sensation overload as he fucked me with his fingers and teased my clit with his wicked tongue.

My climax started in my belly, the muscles there clenching and releasing as I started to feel overwhelmed.

I'd needed him; I'd needed this.

"Yes," I moaned loudly as my impending climax became a whirl of stunning sensation. I closed my eyes, relishing the impending orgasm.

Trace didn't let up. He fucked me harder with his fingers, stimulated my clit with a strength that left me stunned.

"Trace!" I screamed as my climax hit me full-force, rocking my body in its intensity.

I shuddered as I crested, my back arching off the bed as Trace kept up his pace, never giving me any choice but to come hard.

I panted as I spiraled back down, breathless as he lapped at the evidence of my release like he was desperate to taste every drop.

There was no time to recover. He rolled, and I was on top of him instantly, my legs straddling him, my still-throbbing, damp core pressing against his defined abs.

"Take what you want, Eva," Trace rasped. "But for Christ's sake, do it now."

"I want you." My breath was still moving in and out of my lungs at a rapid pace. It wasn't because I hadn't recovered, but because I was still so damn needy, so desperate for Trace to be inside me.

"Then do it. I can't wait much longer."

The fierce desire in his voice spurred me on. I had no idea how to do this, but I was going to find a way. "I'm not sure what I'm doing." Not that I wanted to remind him that I was pretty inexperienced, but I'd need his cooperation.

His hands grasped my ass roughly. "Guide me inside you."

I did what he asked, one hand wrapped around his enormous member as I guided it to my sheath. I let go as he took control, moving me with the pressure he had on my rear end, then forcing me downward.

The stretching sensation was sublime as I slowly lowered my body with his help, gasping as he became totally seated inside me. "Yes." I threw my head back and rolled my hips.

"Now fuck me," Trace said in a graveled voice.

I started to move, him guiding me with his tight grip on my ass.

"Oh, God." I rotated my hips, testing the feel of him in this position, reveling in the pleasure I felt just having our bodies connected.

I melted into him as he held me in place and began to thrust up and into me over and over again.

Each stroke of his hips claimed me, consumed me until I could think of nothing else except slaking our desires. I lowered my upper body, letting my skin slide against his. My nipples were hard and tight, and I drew in a sharp breath as they were almost painfully stimulated as they slid along his damp chest.

I put my hands on either side of his head, looking down at him as he continued a punishing rhythm in and out of my channel. The expression on his face looked strained. I couldn't make out his eyes, but I knew that if it were possible, I'd see them flashing fire.

"You're so damn tight," he growled.

Considering I was almost a virgin, that was highly possible.

"Am I hurting you?" His query was sharp and tortured.

"No. You feel perfect."

I lowered my head and kissed him, tasting myself on his lips. It was erotic, sensual, every movement we made done with carnal heat.

His hand plunged between us, and his fingers strummed over my clit, making me start into another orgasm that I thought might kill me. "I can't. Not again."

"Again," he insisted, groaning as my squeezing sheath started to tighten on his cock. "Fuck. Eva!"

We tumbled over the edge together, our bodies still connected as he released himself inside me.

"So damn good," Trace spat out gutturally.

My heart and body echoed his words, but I couldn't speak. It didn't matter that Trace was literally tutoring me, and I didn't care if the technique wasn't perfect. All that was really important was the overflowing pleasure that spilled from my body and found its way to my heart.

I rested my weight on Trace, both of us gulping for air. In my heart, I knew the moment I got into his bed that I'd sealed my fate, but my attraction to Trace was too fierce, too damn strong for me to resist. I wanted to believe I could just live for today, but I knew tomorrow would come, and I'd pay for the things we'd done with a broken heart.

I was falling in love with Trace Walker.

Maybe I'd never been in love, but I knew what it *wasn't*, and the way I felt about him was different from anything I'd ever experienced before. He was like crack, an addiction that I couldn't turn away from if I could just get my hands on him again.

I let my head rest against his damp shoulder, my body riding with his labored breathing. "I should move." He could breathe a lot better if I'd just move my ass.

His arms tightened around me, his hold like a steel vise. "Don't. You're exactly where I need you to be right now," he insisted huskily.

I sighed and relaxed into his body, feeling safer than I'd ever felt in my entire life. Trace had become the one stable thing in my life, a man who cared. Not that I'd convinced myself that he loved me, but his possessive hold on my body screamed that he wanted me, cared about me. I held tightly to that, trying not to think about the day I'd have to walk away from him.

His lips skimmed my forehead lightly. "Hey, are you okay, sweetheart?" he asked sleepily.

"I'm good," I reassured him. And I wasn't lying. I felt happy, content. As long as I didn't think about the future...

"I'm not sorry you're here. I wanted you to come to me, Eva. But I have to know why."

He let me move to his side, but he gathered my body against his, kept me pressed against his side as he added, "Don't ever leave me." He buried his face in my hair, his grip on my body tight and possessive.

His voice sounded slightly bewildered and vulnerable. My heart squeezed in my chest as I thought about the fact that Trace had his own vulnerabilities. Everybody in his life that he'd cared about had left him. His father, his mother, and to some extent, his siblings. Dane had withdrawn from life, and Sebastian was still trying to figure out who he was with Trace trying to make him grow up faster than he wanted to. In reality, Trace was just as alone as I was, even though he had the money to do whatever he pleased.

He's not happy.

I'd been able to sense his intensity and his restlessness since the moment we'd met. Maybe because I could relate to how he felt.

"This is supposed to be temporary," I whispered to myself, quietly enough so he didn't hear me, even as I drank in Trace's musky scent and the joy I experienced in his arms.

"I'm not going anywhere," I told him in a louder voice.

"Good."

I sighed and let go of the future. Because of Trace, I had things to look forward to, things I never thought I'd have because of my past. I didn't want to spoil the perfection of "now" to think about a doomsday tomorrow.

I snuggled into him and wallowed in the novelty of feeling safe and protected. I relished the fact that he wanted me with him now. In some ways, he needed me just as much as I needed him.

I swore to myself that before I left, I'd make sure Trace could laugh again, that he could connect with his family. I wanted to make him as happy as he'd made me for the last few weeks. He deserved it, and all I had to give was myself, my heart.

His breathing became relaxed and even, and I knew he was asleep. Tilting my head, I kissed his rough jawline and let myself follow him into a comfortable slumber, our bodies locked together like they'd never come apart again.

CHAPTER TWELVE
Trace

S he.
Thump!
Is.
Thump. Thump!
Fucking.
Thump!
Mine.
Thump. Thump. Thump!

I stopped, having beaten the shit out of my bag for over an hour. Unfortunately, it hadn't help curb the raging possessiveness that had been pounding through me since I'd taken Eva the night before.

I was screwed, completely addicted to her, and I would be damned if she ever left. She was like a light to my dark soul, and I was enjoying the illumination and the heat. I fucking needed her now, and I couldn't let her go.

I swiped a gloved hand over my forehead. I was sweating like a pig, but I didn't want to stop venting my frustrations on my pseudo opponent. If I did, I was afraid I'd completely lose it.

"I have to go," I grumbled irritably, grabbing a towel as I headed for the shower.

Eva and I were due to leave the house shortly. I was already committed to attend the company Christmas party, and it wouldn't look good if the boss didn't make an appearance. Honestly, I'd rather stay home and take Eva to bed, fuck her until I came to my senses.

"I can't." My voice was graveled and low as I turned on the cool water of the gym shower while talking to myself. Jesus! I *was* actually talking to myself, carrying on like I was demented.

I entered the cold water without even flinching. I was getting used to it. I'd never needed a cold shower until I'd met *her.* Now, I was becoming unfamiliar with the feeling of warm water.

Stroking my hard cock, all I wanted was to get myself off, but I already knew it wouldn't help. The release never lasted for more than a few minutes. All I had to do was see her and I'd be hard all over again, just like I'd never come.

"Fuck!" I scrubbed my body mercilessly, trying to get the scent of her out of my pores. It didn't work.

It wasn't that I didn't like Eva. Hell, I was obsessed with her. But I didn't like needing anyone, and I sure as hell didn't want to feel like I needed to be with her in order to take my next breath. It was a damned helpless situation to be in, and I fucking hated that, too.

For the first time in a very long time, my emotions were out of control. I'd tried to stay away from her today, certain I'd be able to get my head together. After doing some work in my office, I'd called Dane and Sebastian to see what time they were getting in. Finally, I'd come down here, the only place I could think of to try to get my mind off Eva.

Finished, I turned off the shower, exited the enclosure, and grabbed a towel. As I was hastily drying my body, I wondered what it was about her that wouldn't let me have a single thought that didn't involve both of us naked.

It's not just about sex.

Nope. It wasn't. If my attraction to Eva was purely carnal, it would be waning by now. Instead, it was getting worse. Even now, I was wondering what she was thinking, what she was doing. Most of all, I wanted to be close to her, breathe the same air she was breathing.

I tossed the towel in the open hamper. "I must be fucking crazy," I rasped, afraid for my sanity.

I couldn't push her away; I couldn't be close to her without my emotions going on overload.

Disgusted with myself, I ran upstairs and to my room, not sure if I was disappointed or relieved when I found my bedroom empty. I wanted Eva here. I wanted her to invade my life in the way only a woman could.

I dressed quickly after looking at the clock and realizing I should already be out the door. Not that it really mattered. None of my staff needed me to be able to have a good time at the swanky country club where the festivities were being held.

But I hated being late. I was never late.

I donned my black tuxedo quickly, getting ready in record time. I left the bedroom without a backward glance, not wanting my gaze to land on the enormous king-sized bed where I'd fucked Eva like my life depended on it the night before.

Exiting in a rush, I nearly collided with her as I strode into the hall. I steadied her the moment her body crashed into me.

"I'm sorry I'm late." We spoke the words in unison.

I couldn't help but grin at her as she stepped back.

I reached for the collar of my formal white shirt so I could tug on it, suddenly feeling warm. My eyes devoured Eva, her curvy, feminine body in the same red, *fuck-me* dress that had haunted me since I'd laid eyes on it a few weeks ago. "You're wearing...that?"

Her face fell. "Yes. You said it was formal. Does it look bad on me?"

"No." She looked incredibly sensual, the silky material clinging to her body in places that should probably be illegal. By today's standards, the dress was modest, but I knew it left her back bare, and the graceful line of her neck showing. Too much of her creamy skin was exposed, and I hated it. "You look beautiful."

Her hair was drawn up in an elegant style, secured at the top of her head. Her makeup was perfect, and there wasn't one single thing out of place.

"Thanks." She fidgeted with her dress nervously.

"Don't. You look perfect."

She stopped playing with the garment to look at me, her eyes shining with uncertainly. "Do you really think so? You didn't sound too sure."

"I'm jealous. I don't want any other man to see you in this dress. I'm afraid somebody will steal you away from me." I was honest. I didn't want her to be uncomfortable when she was just finding her confidence.

Her smile was worth my confession. "You're so full of shit," she told me with a laugh. "But I love it."

She took the arm I held out to her, and I led her downstairs, never admitting that I had been completely serious about my fears.

If I'd had any concerns about how Eva would mingle with my employees—which I actually never really did—any doubt would have been dissolved as I watched her from her place next to me at dinner. Her smile was genuine, and her interest in people was sincere. It was like my acquaintances could sense that she was really interested in their lives. And they had no problem talking about themselves.

There was nothing practiced or falsely polite about Eva. People were just naturally drawn to her smile.

I could relate to that. My dick had been continually hard because that smile affected me just that much.

After dinner, people had grouped together, most of them friends from the same area at work, or employees who worked in the same department.

I was trying to look interested in what the Vice President of Walker Corp was saying to me, but I didn't want to hear about work. It was a damn Christmas party for God's sake. Wasn't he capable of shutting the hell up for just five minutes about work issues?

Finally, I held up a hand to silence him. "It's a holiday party, Turner. Can't we leave business behind for one night?"

"Of course, sir," he answered nervously. "I just thought you wanted the numbers on this deal."

I shook my head and looked at the earnest expression on the man's face. He was a hard worker, and an executive in my company. How was it that I knew so little about his life? "Where's your wife, Turner?"

"I'm not sure. I think she's talking to some of the other wives."

"I suggest you go find her and get her a drink." It wasn't really a suggestion. My voice was pretty insistent. "We can discuss business next week. Have fun, Turner. And relax for a while, man. Maybe take some time to appreciate your family."

I knew he had two sons, and a beautiful wife who would do anything for him. He was a lucky guy.

He nodded abruptly. *Smart man.* No wonder I'd made him a VP. "Thank you, sir." He hesitated before adding, "Merry Christmas, Mr. Walker."

Hell, the guy was almost stammering. Was I usually that much of a Scrooge? "Merry Christmas, Turner."

I watched thoughtfully as Turner scrambled away to find his wife. I knew every detail of what my employees did and what they handled at work. I found it strange that I didn't even know how old Turner's kids were. Come to think of it, I knew almost nothing personal about *any* of my executives. Maybe because I'd never bothered to ask. My business functioned like a tightly-run ship, and I was the asshole captain. Generally, this didn't bother me, but as I'd watched Eva learn more personal things about my employees during one dinner than I'd discovered over years of employment, it *was* rather pathetic.

It wasn't that I didn't care about the people who worked for me. But I got so consumed with how efficiently the company ran that I didn't have room in my life for anything more. Or maybe I was afraid of befriending any of them. Oh hell, I didn't know *why* I was an asshole, I just knew that I *was* one.

I took a sip of my Scotch on the rocks and stared at Eva. I was across the room from her, and she was engaged in conversation with some women who were secretaries in the Contract Department. She wasn't paying the least bit of attention to me, but I still felt like she was subconsciously beckoning me, luring me closer to her with every animated movement of her body, every adorable expression on her face.

This was how Eva was born to be: happy, expressive, and friendly to everybody who came into contact with her. It was how her life should have been...but wasn't.

I knew who she'd spotted the minute I saw her expression change. Her arms, which had just been making expressive movements, dropped to her sides and her face became wary, her body tensing as she looked to her right and across the room.

Maybe I shouldn't have invited her here. Maybe it was a mistake.

It killed me to see the light in Eva's eyes dim, but there were things she deserved to know, and I'd invited Mrs. Mitchell here for that specific purpose. She'd begged me to be allowed to talk to Eva in person, but there was no way I was going to let my privacy—and Eva's—be invaded in my home. Eva was safe, and I wanted her to continue to feel that way in my house. But I'd also understood, after finding out the details of Eva's parentage, that she had to know the whole truth.

"Shit! I hope I don't regret this," I rasped in a quiet voice that nobody around me could hear.

I took another slug of my whiskey, watching the two women closely as the older woman made her way through the crowd to Eva. She slowly drew Eva away from the women she was talking to, and I saw a stubborn flash of temper on my sweet girl's face that made me grin.

She can take care of herself.

Yeah, I knew Eva could defend herself, but I wanted to go to her because I knew seeing her accuser was going to make her vulnerable. However, I'd made a promise to Nora Mitchell that she could have a few minutes alone with Eva if she met her here tonight. I wanted Eva to have a neutral place, a venue where it didn't matter if she had bad memories of her discussion with Nora.

I could tell the initial confrontation wasn't going well. Eva looked downright pissed off, and Nora Mitchell looked tearful.

I released a breath I didn't even know I was holding when Nora took Eva's arm lightly and gave her a pleading glance that caused Eva to turn and follow her.

If she hurts Eva, says one word that even upsets her, I vowed that Nora Mitchell would regret it for the rest of her life.

Restlessly, I moved across the room, my eyes unconsciously searching for Eva. I didn't see her, and I knew the two women had found a private place to talk.

I'll wait. I promised to give Nora time.

Honestly, I didn't give a shit about my promise to the older woman, but I was hoping the discussion would give Eva some closure with her past. Ultimately, this was all about Eva for me, and I silently hoped that I'd done the right thing.

CHAPTER THIRTEEN

Eva

*I*t shouldn't have really surprised me to see the woman I hated more than any other female alive show up at a Walker party.

What had really shocked me was when she approached me, asked to have a discussion with me privately. All I could think was that she was going to warn me that she'd expose me if I showed my face in her social circle again.

I braced myself for her lecture as she led me into a small, empty room that was just as plush as the rest of the country club.

"Please sit," the older woman said.

"I'd prefer to stand," I answered rigidly as I pulled my arm from her light grasp. I doubted this would take very long.

"It's a rather lengthy story, Evangelina. Please." She sat on a gold couch and motioned to the matching chair across from her.

Nobody ever called me by my full name, so she got my attention. I perched awkwardly on the edge of the chair, ready to duck out of the room if she started haranguing me.

Who was I kidding? This meeting just made me realize that even though my record was clear, I'd never be free of my past.

Time spent in prison had a way of catching up to a person, whether they were guilty or not. In some people's eyes, I'd always be a thief, a convicted criminal.

My gaze drifted up from their previous position, which had been directed at the floor. I wasn't guilty of anything, and I had no reason to fear this woman anymore. Still, our confrontation made me nauseous.

I barely knew Nora Mitchell, had only met her briefly once before her son's birthday party. She'd never come to my trial, but had given a written statement. Supposedly, she'd been too ill to come in person at the time. She was attractive for a woman her age, which I guessed was probably in her early sixties. Unlike some rich women, she didn't try to cover her age with hair dyes, and her short style was curly and an attractive silvery gray. Her dress was a pretty powder blue, elegant rather than showy, and she was sporting a few pieces of the jewelry that had once been missing, making me flinch as I recognized the gems.

"First, I want to apologize to you. I convicted you without knowing all the facts."

Okay. She shocked me, and I was pretty sure my mouth was hanging open as I gaped at her silently.

She continued, "I didn't want to believe that Karen could steal from me, when it should have been perfectly obvious that she had. All I could think about was protecting her. All I'd ever tried to do was protect her."

"I don't understand." Why would Nora Mitchell care about my mother? She'd been a temporary companion for a very short amount of time.

"Karen was my only child, Evangeline. Your mother was my daughter."

I put a hand on my belly as it began to roll in protest. "That's impossible. My mother said her parents didn't accept her or her pregnancy with me. She said her parents had washed their hands of her."

Mrs. Mitchell shook her head, a remorseful expression on her face. "Your grandfather was a harsh man, and he wasn't an easy man to live with. It's true that he cut Karen off and never spoke to her again, and he didn't allow me to see her either. I looked for you and your mother after he died and I re-married, this time to a kinder husband. But I couldn't locate her. Eventually, I convinced myself that I was better off not knowing."

That statement hurt because I didn't understand how someone could so easily forget that she had a child and grandchild somewhere in the world, but I let the emotion pass. It didn't matter anymore, and I was still trying to wrap my head around her claims. "Did she know who you were when she came to work for you?"

Nora nodded. "She knew, but she said she didn't want me to give her anything. She was just there for a job. Since I couldn't connect with her any other way, I let her take the position. I wanted to meet you, which is why she brought you to work at my stepson's birthday party."

"Stepson?" I hadn't known he wasn't her natural son.

"I have three stepchildren. Two boys and a girl. I love them all like they're my own. But I never forgot your mother."

Resentment started to rise from the pit of my stomach, but I pushed it back down. "But you apparently forgot you had a granddaughter," I answered drily.

"I didn't, Evangelina. Even after I'd convinced myself you were guilty, I wasn't ever going to say a word, but I had to."

Well, that explained why it had taken some time for Mrs. Mitchell to realize the jewelry was gone. "You were going to cover for me?"

She nodded, her gray head bobbing nervously. "Just like I always did for your mother."

"What do you mean?"

"Your mother was never an easy child, and she became an even wilder teenager. If she got in trouble, I helped her and never told her father. Later, after she'd left and her father had passed away, I started reading a lot of literature on mental health. I'd say she was probably bipolar, and had some other issues from being raised by my first husband. He was abusive, both mentally and physically. I blame myself for that. I stayed with him, and Karen had to live with the abuse."

"Are you making excuses for her?" I asked bitterly, knowing I had no place in my heart to forgive my mother.

"Not anymore. I just want you to understand what happened to her."

"My father was a good man. He worked long hours to keep a roof over our head. We might not have had the material things like she did when she lived at home, but my father loved her, even when she treated him like dirt." Mostly, that was the only way my mother had *ever* treated my father.

"I never met him, but I'm sure he was a good man. But your mother's father was very conscious of his image, and he refused to have her unwed and pregnant in our house. I know it wasn't right, and I felt so helpless when he threw her out when she was pregnant, but maybe I was hoping she'd be better off out of the house." What Mrs. Mitchell didn't mention was the fact that I was a mixed-race child. But she didn't have to. It was obvious that had I been of a better pedigree, I would have been more readily accepted.

"She never changed. She was just as crazy out of your home as she was when she lived there. Maybe she was bipolar, but she was also sociopathic. Everything was all about her, and if things didn't go her way, she made everybody around her miserable."

"I figured that out after some time in her company as my companion," Mrs. Mitchell agreed. "I begged her to get treatment for her mental health issues, but she refused."

"Why in the world did you let her hook up with Trace's father?" No man had deserved my mother, and by all accounts from Trace, his dad had been a good man.

"I felt guilty for the life Karen had lived when she was younger. I thought maybe if she made a good marriage, she'd get better," Mrs. Mitchell said contritely.

"She was selfish, she was a thief, and she was a liar. Trace's father didn't deserve getting stuck with her without knowing exactly what he was getting into."

"I know all of those things, but it didn't erase the fact that she was my baby girl, my only child. I made excuses for her when she was younger. I think I was still trying to make her a better woman than she really was. Of all people, I knew she wasn't right in the head. But I didn't want to admit it."

Tears of remorse was running down Nora Mitchell's face, but as I thought about the stone cold fear that I'd lived in for most of my adult life, I had a very hard time feeling sympathy for her. "So I could be sacrificed to protect her?" I asked flatly.

"No. And you shouldn't have been. But it took me a long time to be honest with myself."

I gritted my teeth. "When? When did you decide to see the truth?"

Nora dug into the large purse she was carrying and pulled something from inside. "When Trace came to me for answers, I finally read her journal. She left it at my house when she went to marry your father. Trace showed me the video, and he told what he believed to be true. He was right."

I stared at the plain black notebook. She was offering it to me, but I wasn't sure I wanted to take it.

She dropped it on the small coffee table that separated us. "I'm so sorry, Evangelina. I should have always known it was Karen. But I thought she was going to marry Trace's father and everything would go right for her."

"What about me?"

"I convinced myself you were guilty, and that you deserved to spend time in prison."

"I didn't do it. I've never stolen anything in my life except discarded food occasionally." I'd done what I had to do to survive, but I'd always hated it. Even if it was garbage, I knew it wasn't *my* garbage, and I shouldn't be taking anything that didn't belong to me. But survival was a strong instinct to fight.

"I understand. I don't expect you to forgive me, but I wanted you to know that I was sorry." The woman broke down in tears, one of her hands fisted to cover her mouth as though she wanted to hide the fact that she was crying.

I watched as fat tears dripped down her cheeks, and my heart started to bleed. I stood and walked over to her chair. I crouched down and took the hand that was lying on her leg. "She's not worth it, you know."

"Who?" Mrs. Mitchell's voice was scratchy.

"My mother. She's not worth the pain that you carry inside you. She probably never was."

"I'm not crying for her," she answered tearfully. "I'm sad for you."

I didn't want this woman's pity. "Don't. I'm safe now. Trace has helped me in ways nobody else could or would. He trusted me."

"Trace Walker is a good man, Evangelina." She stroked the diamond on my finger. "I'm glad that you're going to be happy. It was pretty obvious to me that he loves you."

I swallowed a denial, realizing that Trace had never told her the truth about our engagement. He didn't love me, but he did care. "He's an intense man," I answered noncommittally.

Nora sniffled. "Sometimes those are the best kind. I've buried two husbands now. And I know the difference between a good and a bad relationship."

"Did Trace set up this meeting?" I was pretty convinced that Nora being here was more than a coincidence.

"Yes. He didn't like it, but he agreed that you should know the truth."

"The truth shall set you free," I murmured, doubting how right that biblical quote was in my situation. "I'm glad you told me."

I stood up and placed her hand gently back on her thigh.

"I'm sorry," she muttered again.

I looked down at her and realized she was just as much a victim as I had been. Though her motivation was skewed, she'd been trying to right her wrongs. She didn't have to be here telling me the truth. She could have been in denial for the rest of her life, letting me forever take the blame in her mind. It would have been easier, and kinder to her psyche.

"It's okay," I told her softly. "I survived."

"You should have had so much more than survival."

I picked up my mother's journal, knowing I had to read it. "I did. I had my father for fourteen years. He was more than enough."

"You really loved him," Mrs. Mitchell stated.

I nodded. "I really did. Thank you for telling me the truth."

"I'd like to be part of your life someday, Evangelina. You've grown into an amazing woman."

At one time, I would have given anything to hear that from family. Now, my mind was cluttered with information, and I was still trying to process the details I'd been given. "I need time to think."

The older woman nodded her head once. "Of course. Call me after you've had time to think it over. I'll understand if you don't." She nodded her head at my mother's journal. "It's going to be hard to read. She was very angry."

I walked to the door and twisted the handle. "It's nothing I'm not used to," I informed her, then walked out the door.

Trace was there to support me, his arm around my waist. "Are you okay?"

His expression was unreadable, but I knew he was asking if I could accept what I'd just been told. "I don't know."

Escorting me to the elevator, he didn't say a word to me or anyone else on the way out.

I waited until the elevator doors closed us in alone before I hurled myself into his arms and cried.

CHAPTER FOURTEEN

Eva

I started to panic as the door slowly began to close, the bars appearing in front of my face before the door completely shut and locked me in with a loud bang. The finality of the sound echoed the resignation in my soul.

I was going to spend years in this place, pay for a crime I never would have committed.

Heart racing, I tried to stifle my hysteria as I lifted my hands and grasped the bars.

I didn't do this!

I need to get out!

I didn't belong here, but fairness had no place in my fate.

It wasn't like I hadn't been here before. I'd had to be locked up to await my trial. But this was different. I was no longer waiting for release because I'd been found innocent.

I'd been found guilty, and sentenced to four years. How in the hell had this happened?

Terror gripped me with clammy hands, and a chill ran down my spine.

I wasn't getting out.

I wasn't getting out for a very long time.

My situation was surreal, but the reality was sinking in fast.

"I didn't do it," I whispered frantically to myself, but words were futile. There hadn't been a single person who'd believed I was innocent. From now on, even when I got out, I'd be a convicted felon.

"No. Please. I didn't do it." My voice got louder, more hysterical.

Sobs of desperation escaped my mouth, and I slid down to my knees, my hands sliding down the bars, feeling hopeless.

"No! No! No!" I screamed, hoping somebody would listen, that somebody might care. "Noooooo!"

"Eva!" A stern, masculine voice pierced my foggy, panicked brain.

"Trace?" Tears were flowing down my face and my body was trembling as I sat up in bed.

"Jesus! I didn't think you were ever going to wake up." He wrapped his arms around my naked body.

A dream. It was just a dream. I was out of prison, and Traced believed I was innocent. In fact, he'd proved it.

I relaxed into his body, still a little confused in the dark bedroom, although I knew that we were in his bed. "I'm sorry," I mumbled against his naked chest.

"Bad dreams?"

I nodded, even though I knew he couldn't see me. "Yes. I haven't had nightmares for a while now." I was guessing that seeing Nora had triggered the pain that was still buried deep inside me.

"About your prison sentence?"

"Yes. I was terrified when I first got locked up. I couldn't believe it was really happening."

"You thought the justice system would never be wrong?"

"For some reason, I trusted that they'd find out the truth. But they never really looked for it. It was pretty likely that I was guilty, so nobody really bothered." I wasn't sure I could really blame them. The case had looked pretty clear cut and simple.

"This is about your grandmother, isn't it?" Trace asked huskily.

"Kind of...yes. But she thought I was guilty, too."

"Fuck! I should have just told her no. I shouldn't have forced this on you."

"No, you shouldn't have. I was angry at you, but I understand why you did it. If you had asked, I would have refused. And I think I needed to hear her story."

When Trace and I left the party, I hadn't said much. Although I'd initially leaned on him, I ended up angry that he'd set me up to see Mrs. Mitchell. I'd undressed myself and slid into his bed while he lagged behind. Emotionally exhausted, I'd fallen asleep before he'd come to bed.

"That last thing I'd wanted was to cause you more pain, Eva." His voice was remorseful as he subconsciously soothed me by rubbing my back.

"I know." I sighed, knowing that Trace was used to doing what he thought best. "But I'd like some warning before you ever pull something like that again."

"Done." His agreement was immediate.

He lowered me back to my pillow, and my eyes fluttered closed.

"Sleep, sweetheart. We'll talk about it tomorrow." He laid an arm over my waist possessively.

Because I was still wiped out, I obeyed his command and slept.

When I opened my eyes again, it was still dark. For an instant, I wondered why I'd awoken so abruptly, but it only took me a moment to understand that it had been my aroused body that refused to keep on sleeping.

Oh, my God.

I could feel Trace's heated, rock-hard body against my back, a sizeable erection resting against my bare ass. He had pulled me into his body. Hard. One of his hands rested solidly against my belly. The other...

Oh, shit!

I stifled a moan, my body tensing as his marauding fingers teased my clit lazily. He was exploring my pussy like it belonged to him, like it was an extension of his own body. I wasn't sure if he was completely awake.

"Don't tell me to stop." Trace's voice was husky with desire.

I guess my question of whether or not he was sleeping was answered. I shivered as his warm breath wafted against the sensitive skin of my neck and ear.

God, he felt good.

Not sure how I even felt about Trace right now, I didn't respond verbally. My body wanted him, but my brain was still angry that he'd set me up without asking me if I even wanted to see the woman who had been my accuser. While my logical brain might understand his decision, I couldn't help but feel slightly...betrayed.

My breath hitched as I stared into the darkness, my body pleading with my mind to give in to Trace.

"I know you're awake, Eva."

Of course he knew I was awake. I was starting to pant like a wanton sex maniac.

"I know you need me right now," Trace rasped.

My back arched as he began to get serious about making me come. "Please," I breathed softly as my body tensed, my climax rapidly approaching as he stroked over the tiny bundle of nerves faster and faster. Harder and harder.

If he was trying to prove that I needed him, he was succeeding.

"Come for me," he demanded against my neck, his mouth exploring the sensitive skin there as his other hand came up to my breasts and teased the stiff peaks of my nipples.

I was drowning in sensation, all thoughts of anything except satisfaction fleeing my mind. My body was in control, and it needed Trace.

I raised my top leg and rested it behind me, stretching it over Trace's thighs to give him all the access he needed to drive me crazy.

"Good girl," he whispered soothingly. "Let me in."

I had a fleeting thought that his words meant more than just me making the erotic task he'd undertaken easier for him, but I was too far gone into my haze of pleasure to analyze what he had said.

My head fell back against his shoulder and I felt so vulnerable in that moment, so raw that it was almost frightening.

Trace could play me like an instrument, and I responded so easily, so naturally.

My orgasm washed over me in a wave of ecstasy that heightened and then rippled over every nerve in my body, leaving me spent and relaxed in his arms as I moaned through my climax.

I laid there for a while, Trace holding me tightly, his hand moving to stroke my bare hip before asking, "Feel better?"

"Hmm..." My capacity to speak hadn't entirely returned.

"You were restless. I thought..."

I didn't remember having any more bad dreams, but maybe I hadn't been sleeping well. "And you thought an orgasm might help?" I couldn't help it. I smiled into the darkness.

"No. I held you against my body, then I couldn't help myself." There was a touch of mischievous humor in his voice. "I had to make you come."

"Why?" Nearly recovered, I turned in his arms to face him.

"I couldn't sleep. I wanted to watch over you. I guess now I know that I can't hold you that close and not touch you."

I breathed in his masculine scent as I buried my face into his neck. Jesus! How was it that he always made these declarations just when I wanted so much to be indignant?

"You haven't slept? You've been awake?" I lifted my head to look at the clock. It was almost five a.m. I assumed some hours had passed since I'd woke up from my nightmare.

"No. I know I did the right thing, but I feel like an asshole. It obviously disturbed you."

"It was just a bad dream. My issue is that you didn't talk to me. I had a right to know."

"If had told you, would you have met with Nora?"

I was quiet for moment before replying, "I don't know. But I should have been given the option. I've had my choices taken away from me for years, Trace. Do you know what it's like to be given no basic choices, to be told when to sleep, when to eat, when to work, when to take a pee, for God's sake?"

Deep in my heart, I knew he hadn't made the decision to be in control, even though he *was* a control freak. He'd done it because he'd known that I'd refuse to see Mrs. Mitchell. Honestly, I did know that would have been my choice. I would have shied away from that part of my life because all I wanted to do was forget it.

"I didn't think about that, Eva."

I rolled my eyes in the still-dark room. To give him credit, I *did* assume he was thinking about it *now.*

"It would be Hell," he decided.

"It was worse than that. It was dehumanizing." My experience was the reason I still didn't quite know who I was or where I fit into the world. I'd never had the chance to find out. "I doubt you've ever lost control."

Trace had always been in the situation to decide his own destiny. I hadn't. Ever.

He rolled onto his back and pulled my upper body on top of his chest. As he situated my head on his chest, he answered unhappily, "Not until I met you."

My heart skipped a beat, and I wondered if he was saying I could make him lose control. I'd never really seen it, but I'd like to. "So you're human after all, Mr. Walker," I teased, my irritation starting to fade.

"So it seems," he said drily.

He'd made a hard decision, and although I didn't agree with what he'd done, Trace had picked the most difficult option because he thought it would be best for me. I could forgive him. After all, nobody had ever cared about me enough to even bother themselves to think about my welfare.

I stroked a hand across his chest, savoring the feel of his warm skin over hardened muscle. Then, I let my hand smooth slowly over his abdomen until I could run a finger along the light trail of hair that led to what I already knew was an impressive cock. I smiled as I wrapped my hand around him, not surprised that he was more than a handful.

"Eva. Don't start anything," he rasped bossily.

"Why?" I answered innocently as I stroked him, fascinated by the feel of the soft head of his penis, and the satiny skin stretched over his hard phallus. "You feel incredible."

I'd never groped a guy before, and I was enjoying the feel of Trace.

"I'll lose it," he groaned desperately.

Hell, that was the whole point. I wanted him out of control for once. "I'll make you come," I promised, even though I had no idea whether I could do it or not.

"Fuck!"

His needy curse convinced me to try. There was nothing I wanted more than to taste his pleasure. I moved my mouth down his body, dragging my tongue along his tight abs, delighting at the salty taste of his skin.

Boldly, I kicked the covers down to the bottom of the bed, and moved my mouth to his engorged cock. I licked the mushroom head, and I moaned softly at the taste of the droplet of moisture I swallowed. It was the essence of Trace, and he was absolutely delicious.

I didn't care when he grasped my hair. "I need you to take me into your mouth, Eva." His voice was already desperate and demanding.

"You need me?" I asked, wrapping my hand tighter around the root of his cock. I wanted to hear the same thing he did when he'd been pleasuring me.

"More than I've ever fucking needed anything." His voice was low and feral, scratchy and hoarse.

My heart soared, and that was all I wanted to hear. I wrapped my lips around his cock and took as much of him between my lips as I could handle.

I might be unskilled and inexperienced, but it wasn't like I hadn't heard and read about sex acts for years. I tightened my lips around him and sucked as I pulled back, only to have him push my head forward to take him again almost immediately.

I let him tutor me this time, use his grip on my hair and the strength of his hand to tell me what he wanted. And Trace wasn't shy.

"Suck me harder, Eva. Fuck! I'm not going to last."

He set a brutally fast pace, his hips coming up to fuck my mouth as his hand pressed my face forward. The entire experience was carnal and raw, and I cherished every untamed moment of him as he cursed and groaned his approval.

"Christ. You're making me crazy, Eva. I'm going to come like a fucking horny teenager." He sounded like he was struggling to breathe.

I didn't care how he came, I just wanted it to happen. I wanted to give him the same ecstasy I'd experienced a short time ago.

Do it. Come for me, Trace.

I took my free hand and gently fondled his balls, and his body tensed.

"Move back unless you want a mouthful," he warned urgently.

I did. I wanted it. I wanted to experience every single part of Trace. I wrapped my lips around him harder, even though he was nudging my head away from his pulsating cock, and then I took as much of him as I could, plus a little bit more.

"Dammit, Eva!" he groaned desperately, his back coming off the bed as he seemed to be in a battle...with himself. "You feel too damn good."

I felt the rush of his hot release in the back of my throat as he stopped trying to fight with himself, and I swallowed happily. His reaction was exquisite, the moment almost surreal.

Trace Walker was completely lost in his release, his grip on my hair wild and almost painful as he spilled himself with an abandon I'd never experienced before.

His body relaxed and he flopped back down on the bed. I could hear his labored breathing as his grip on my head relaxed.

I savored the experience, licking him clean as he struggled to take in air, then crawled slowly up beside him.

"I warned you," he said harshly, his voice raw.

"I know. I wanted to taste you," I answered honestly as I laid on my stomach next to him and arranged a pillow under my head.

Although I knew that it was going to be painful when my job with Trace was over, I wanted to experience everything I could while I was with him. I'd been deprived of feeling anything but fear and devastation for so long that I couldn't resist taking any kind of joy I could experience, even if I'd pay for it later.

I felt him sit up and reach for the sheet and quilt at the end of the bed. I squealed as his hand came down on my bare ass with a *whack!*

"What was that for?" I asked in a faux outraged voice.

"For driving me crazy," he grumbled as he covered our bodies and gathered me close to him, making me abandon my pillow for his shoulder.

I smiled as he tucked the covers around me protectively. "I'd say it was a pretty short drive. You hired your stepsister to be your fiancée, and she ends up being a convict. But you still didn't run away." I was teasing him, but really, maybe he was just a little bit off the rails.

"You're not a convict, and I'd never run away from you. I need you too damn much." He sounded completely serious, and somewhat disgruntled.

That shut me up. My heart might be rejoicing, but I knew I couldn't make too much out of his admission.

I need you, too.

The thought jumped into my mind, but I closed my mouth so I didn't say it aloud. If I'd learned anything in my rough background, it was that there were very few people in life I could count on long term except myself.

Closing my eyes, I let myself enjoy just being in his arms, his arms protectively enclosing me. For now, I felt safe, and that had to be enough.

CHAPTER FIFTEEN

Trace

"I'm still trying to figure out how you scored a woman who can cook as well as Eva," Sebastian Walker said nonchalantly as he tossed back a whiskey in one gulp.

I hadn't realized how much I missed Sebastian and Dane until they'd arrived for Christmas. Having Britney around made things tense, but my youngest brother didn't seem to be hopelessly in love with her. At least I hoped he wasn't.

Eva had been amazing, cooking delicious meals and charming my brothers until I swore they were both half in love with her, which annoyed the hell out of me. To be honest, she was just being herself, but that was enough to make them both intrigued, especially since she wasn't exactly the type of woman I usually dated. "I'm a lucky guy," I replied, looking at both my brothers sitting on opposite sides of the couch in the living room from my seat across from them.

Eva had disappeared after dinner, claiming that she needed to wrap some gifts before retreating upstairs. Britney had said she was tired, and she'd disappeared also, not that I was heartbroken. I'd seen enough of the poisonous bitch to last a lifetime.

It was Christmas Eve, and I'd succeeded in never being alone with Britney for a single minute. Eva had stayed by my side, playing the part of the adoring fiancée so well that I was starting to get used to it. I can't lie. I loved every minute of her being mine, even though it was a façade.

"You're very lucky, Trace," Dane agreed in a low, thoughtful voice. "It's not easy finding a woman who doesn't care if you're rich and doesn't just want you for your money. I think you can safely say that Eva doesn't give a damn. I can tell she just wants you to be happy."

I gaped at him, wondering why Dane thought *that.* It nearly killed me, but I had to ask him. "Is that the way it is with Britney?"

"Not even remotely," Dane answered casually.

"You don't think she loves you?" Sebastian asked, frowning as he rose to pour himself another drink.

I continued to stare at Dane, wondering what was going on in his head. Did he know that Britney was using him?

"Britney is convenient. She's willing to stay on the island for what I can give her, and she tolerates letting me fuck her. Do either of you think I don't know she's using me?" He looked at Sebastian and I curiously.

Hell, my younger brother was way smarter than I gave him credit for. "Then why do you keep her?"

Dane shrugged. "Who else is going to have me? I wanted to get laid, and she was willing to suffer through it if I gave her enough to make up for the inconvenience. I don't have any fantasies that she cares about anything more than money. She never has."

There was some bitterness in Dane's voice, but I was relieved that he wasn't going to be heartbroken when Britney decided it was time to leave. In fact, it was more than likely that Dane would get tired of her whining and ask her to leave himself.

Sebastian flopped back onto the couch with a full glass. "Dude, no offense, but Britney is annoying as hell, even if she is a fine looking woman."

I smiled, realizing that Sebastian had finally seen through Britney's blonde hair and cornflower blue eyes, discovering that there was nothing inside to match the beauty of her exterior.

Dane shrugged. "No offense taken. She's a raving bitch, and I know it. I think I'm starting to prefer being lonely to having her around." He turned his head. "Is that what happened with you two, Trace?"

I nearly choked on my drink. *Fuck! He knows.*

"What?" I lowered my drink from my mouth with a cough.

"Did you get sick of her, too? Is that why you dumped her?"

I let out a huge breath. "How did you know I dated her?"

Dane's lips smiled, but his eyes were sad. "I might live on an island, but I do get the media. I made sure you and Britney were done before I allowed her to come to the island. I felt kind of bad picking up with a female my brother had broken up with, but it isn't like I have a huge variety of women to choose from. I'm sorry."

"Don't be sorry," I said in a rush. "It wasn't serious between us."

He nodded. "I know."

I shook my head at the irony that I was trying to protect Dane while he'd been sorry he'd dated a woman I'd been with in the past.

"I didn't know you dated Britney." Sebastian sounded pissed. "Why didn't you say something?"

"Maybe because I never catch you sober enough to mention it." My tone was sarcastic and accusing. I regretted saying the words almost immediately, but I couldn't take them back. In reality, I'd deliberately avoided telling Sebastian the truth.

I watched as Sebastian's face went dark, and he took a large swig of his full drink. "At least I don't have a stick up my ass the size of a giant redwood," he mumbled bitterly. "I'm sorry that I'm not as perfect as you are, brother."

I didn't consider myself that uptight. "I'm not asking you to be perfect. I'm just asking you to try to be better. Stop partying all the time for a living."

"I don't need to make a living. I'm a billionaire. You took Dad's place, so what do you expect me to do?"

"You went to college, Sebastian. I expect you to grow up." I was angry now, sick of him criticizing me for something that I had to do.

"Why? I'll never measure up to your expectations. Why try?"

"I don't have expectations. I'm not Dad."

I looked at Dane, but he didn't look ready to jump into the conversation. In fact, he looked perfectly happy to let me fight this out with Sebastian.

"Then quit acting like Dad," Sebastian answered bitterly.

My anger started to boil. "I can never be him. I never could. I fucking tried, but I could never be quite as smooth. I could never be quite as wise, and I sure as hell will never run Walker as well as he did."

"You do amazingly well, Trace," Dane said encouragingly, finally deciding to enter the conversation. "You were young when you took over the company."

"I took it over because I had to. I was the only one old enough to do it. I thought I was the only one who wanted to do it." I glared at Sebastian. "If you wanted to take on that responsibility, why in the hell didn't you say something?"

"Why didn't you ask?" he threw back at me angrily.

I exploded. "Do you think I fucking wanted this? Do you think I wanted to step into Dad's shoes after he died? I was only twenty-one years old, and I didn't have a clue what I was doing. I was stumbling in the dark, trying to finish school while I tried to do his job as the CEO of Walker. I. Wasn't. Fucking. Ready."

I didn't think I'd ever say those words, much less to my brothers. But we were all grown up, and the time for distance between us had to end. We were all broken, and I wanted to see us back in one piece again.

"I'm not that much younger than you. I could have helped," Sebastian broke the silence, his voice no longer angry.

"All I wanted was for you and Dane to have a chance to grieve, a chance to recover and lead a normal life." I knew I was breathing hard, trying to get my emotions under control.

"Our life was never going to be normal again," Dane answered gravely. "I guess we both thought you wanted your position as CEO and you wanted us out of the family business. I was relieved to tell you the truth. I didn't want to be a businessman. It was never something I wanted."

I knew that. I thought Sebastian wanted something else, too. I stared at my second oldest sibling thoughtfully as I asked, "And you? What did you want?"

"I wanted my brothers," Sebastian answered hoarsely. "I wanted Dad back."

"I wanted that, too. But so many people were depending on me that I knew I had to keep everything under control."

"You thought you had to stay distant to keep yourself going?" Dane queried.

"Yes. I was on pretty shaky ground for a while, but I didn't want anyone to know." I'd been terrified, but I didn't admit that. "I still miss Dad every single day," I confessed.

"We all do," Dane answered. "I think we just handle it differently. For a while, I felt guilty that I lived and he died."

Sebastian and I both stared at Dane with astonished expressions. My baby brother had been through so damn much. It irked me that he was also dealing with guilt over being alive when our father was gone. "Don't, Dane," I requested.

My little brother held up a hand. "I got over that. But it took time. Unfortunately, I think Sebastian has some issues to settle."

"I don't—"

I interrupted Sebastian. "I'm sorry. I'm sorry I never asked what either one of you wanted. I assumed too much. I was overwhelmed."

"Not an issue for *me*," Dane answered, staring directly at Sebastian. "Like I said, I was grateful you took over."

Sebastian set his drink on the table and let out a large sigh. "I wasn't grateful. I was jealous. I wanted to be able to be like you, Trace. I wanted to help you, I wanted to be grown up enough to help."

"Don't wish for that," I grunted. "It sucked."

For years, I'd closed off every emotion I had just to keep control. Eva had been the only one to break through my veneer of calm assurance to see me for exactly who I was. I'd never grieved for my father, and I'd never gotten over everything I'd lost.

"You're right, Trace. I do need to grow up," Sebastian admitted as he leaned back against the couch.

"What do you want to do when you grow up?" I asked jokingly.

Sebastian grinned. "Maybe be second in command at Walker? I'm thinking maybe I could buy back in again."

The last thing my brother would ever be is second at anything. "I'd only accept an equal partnership. You'd have to cough up the money to be a partner."

Sebastian had studied engineering, and I'd always assumed he'd start his engineering firm. He had, after all, minored in business. Really, he'd make an incredible partner if he gave up the booze and partying.

"I could take some of the load off of you, Trace," Sebastian said hesitantly. "I think I'd like that. I could head up some of the building projects."

"I hate that part," I told him with a frown.

Sebastian grinned. "Sounds like it might work."

"I'm not moving the main offices back to Texas." I'd worked for too long to get everything centered in Denver, and I liked it here.

"I'll sell the property there and work here," Sebastian compromised.

"It won't be easy," I warned, knowing it would be hard to sell the assets he had in Texas, including the family mansion back near Dallas that Sebastian currently owned and lived in—when he was actually home.

"I don't need easy," Sebastian rasped adamantly. "I just need a purpose."

"You have one," I answered quickly, knowing I wanted my brother with me again. I could see his determination, and I had no doubt he could clean up his act.

Sebastian nodded. "I think I do now."

I looked at both of my brothers, wondering how I could ever have been so misdirected when it came to Sebastian. Had I done the same with Dane?

As though he could hear my thoughts, Dane remarked drily, "Don't be thinking I'll be moving here to Denver. I like my solitude."

Okay. Maybe I'd been on target when it came to Dane.

"I'll start working on selling everything off and moving right after the holidays," Sebastian said eagerly.

I had to grin at his enthusiasm, and my heart felt lighter than it had in years. "So you're ready to dump your social life?"

I noticed Sebastian's whiskey was sitting idle, and he wasn't reaching for it eagerly. I hadn't seen him take a break on drinking since he'd gotten here.

"It was getting boring," he answered earnestly. "I'm thinking I might find myself a woman like Eva, settle down eventually."

"Touch her and brother or not, I'll kill you," I growled, only partially serious.

Sebastian raised a hand in surrender. "She's obviously in love with you. If she wasn't so hung up on your ass, I'd probably try to lure her away. She makes incredible pasta."

"She's more than just a good cook," I said irritably. "She's my everything."

I realized that I wasn't acting anymore. Eva had come to mean so damn much to me in such a short time. Separating after the holidays were over wasn't even an option anymore. I needed her, and I didn't want to imagine what my life would be without her. I think I'd known from the very beginning that I was never going to let her go.

"That's pretty intense," Sebastian mumbled. "I don't think I'll ever meet a woman I can't live without."

"I didn't think so either," I confessed. "But sometimes there's nothing that can stop you from feeling that way."

Hell, I'd tried. I'd beaten up my punching bag until every muscle in my body was screaming, but it hadn't flung Eva out of my soul.

"Better you than me," Sebastian countered. "I don't want to feel that way."

"Me either," Dane added. "How did you guys meet anyway?"

There was nothing I wanted more at that moment than to confess everything about Eva and me. But I couldn't. We were still trying to put our relationship back together again, and I didn't want to ruin the progress we'd made by telling them that I'd set everything up with Eva. Besides, like it or not, she was going to be mine.

"Long story," I answered simply. "But she's never had it easy, and she deserves to be happy."

"I like her," Sebastian said openly.

"Me, too," Dane added.

I nodded, glad that they liked Eva because they'd be seeing her with me forever.

Convincing Eva to stay might not be easy, but I'd make her love me, and she'd never want to leave. It didn't matter how hard I had to work to get her to stay. It would be worth it if I could just keep her forever.

What if she doesn't want to stay? You had an agreement, and she can insist on you honoring it. She's done her part.

Just the thought of Eva saying goodbye made me crazy. I decided not to think about failure, because it wasn't an option.

She'd stay. She'd never leave. She'd be mine fucking forever.

Maybe she'd fight the inevitable, but somehow I'd make her see that we belonged together.

And, in the end, I'd win.

I wasn't as cocky about Eva as I was about business. She was more than business to me now, and she probably had been since the moment she'd boldly walked into my office.

But I *would* win.

I *had* to in order to save my sanity now.

CHAPTER SIXTEEN

Eva

"*I've hated my daughter since the day she was born, but she's finally going to pay for keeping me away from all of the things I should have had. I was born rich, and I should have always been rich. It was my birthright. She's going to jail to pay the price for taking everything away from me. I'm happy. She'll finally be exactly where she should be—which is rotting in prison. It doesn't matter that I committed the crime she's going to be doing time for. So what if I stole the jewelry? It belonged to my mother. It was mine to steal. The important thing is that Eva pays, and I'm pretty sure she'll be convicted. I'm getting back what I deserve by marrying a rich man. I shouldn't have had to marry him to get what I'm entitled to have, but I'll take what I can get now. I wonder if it's wrong to hope that my dead husband's brat dies while she's in prison. I don't think it is, and I hope she never gets out of there alive after they find her guilty.*"

I slammed my mother's journal closed, unable to read another word of her crazy ramblings. It had been her last entry in her journal, a passage written right before her death. I swiped at my tears, wishing I'd never opened the notebook.

My heart clenched in my chest, and I let the pain of my mother's betrayal wash over me, wishing the book had stayed out of my sight.

What had I been hoping for when I opened it to the last entry? That she'd confessed that she really loved me, and that she felt guilty for what she'd done? *No possibility of that after what I'd read.*

The book had been out on Trace's bed when I'd come upstairs to wrap his gift. I could only assume the cleaning crew had found it under the bed and left it on top of the quilt.

Curiously, I'd opened it and read several passages, including the one I'd just stopped reading. It wasn't like Nora hadn't warned me, but I hadn't been ready for the complete and utter evil that had been my mother, the bitter hatred she'd harbored for me all of those years.

"I'm surprised she let me live," I muttered softly, my voice still tearful.

Why she hadn't killed me when I was young I'd never understand. Did she draw the line at murder? Or had she known that she'd never get away with it? She'd certainly wished I was dead. But apparently she'd never had the guts to off me herself. It wasn't out of any sense of mercy. That was clear from her journal entries. More than likely, she was afraid she'd end up in jail for murder.

She's not worth my tears.

In my rational mind, I knew she'd been crazy and I wasn't responsible for her feelings. But the child that still lived inside of me wondered why she could never love me. I'd twisted myself inside out to gain even a tiny crumb of affection from her. When I was a kid, I hadn't understood why she hated me, and I thought it had been my fault. As an adult, I knew better, but for some reason, her hatred for me still hurt.

"It was interesting reading...that little book." The female voice sounded from the doorway.

Britney.

I tried not to gag at her saccharine sweet tone. I knew underneath her gorgeous, blonde supermodel appearance, there was a heart of a viper.

I turned to see her staring at the book in my hand. "What?"

She glided into the room with a conniving smile on her face that I instantly wanted to bitch slap off her face.

I'd avoided being near her when I could, and ignored her nasty jabs at me when I had to be in her company. I like Trace's brothers, and my heart bled for Dane. They might be together, but Britney didn't deserve Dane. Yes, he was scarred, but he didn't deserve another thorn in his side or a pain in the ass like this woman. She was as cold as Antarctica.

"Oh, I hope you don't mind, but I went in search of something to read, and I found that little book in your hands. It was very interesting reading. I think people would be fascinated to learn that Trace Walker is marrying a criminal, and that his father had been duped into marrying a psycho. The whole family story would be a total turnoff, I think. After all, he's marrying his stepsister." Britney's expression turned into an evil smile.

Bitch!

She deliberately snooped and found my mother's journal. I hadn't read it all, but apparently Britney had. "You stole my personal things?" I asked angrily.

I glared at her heavily made-up face, and the long blonde tresses that always looked perfect. Even when we were casually at home, she was dressed like she was going to a party. Today she was dressed in heels and a green mini dress that bared most of her thighs, even though it was probably below freezing outside.

Britney shrugged. "I was looking for reading material. I came across the information by coincidence. You have to admit that it won't be a pretty story. Trace engaged to his criminal stepsister, and his dad fooled into marrying a woman who was certifiable. Trace would have been so much better off with me," Britney mused.

"He'd never be better off with a bitch like you," I growled.

Britney let out a fake gasp. "The kitten's claws are beginning to show. I guess you get rather violent after being in prison. Even you have to admit that it's a little sick to be engaged to your stepsister."

"We. Aren't. Related." I wasn't about to explain my relationship with Trace. It was none of her business.

"Let's just get down to business, shall we?" All traces of innocence were gone from Britney's voice, and she was shedding her superficial snake skin. "Trace belongs with me. I can't screw that freak of a brother of his anymore. I can't even let him touch me. He's hideous. I can't even do it for his money. He makes my skin crawl."

"*You* make *my* skin crawl," I rasped, so angry that I could barely contain myself.

"You're just jealous," Britney rationalized. "I'm beautiful and you know it."

You're ugly on the inside where it counts.

I didn't answer. I simply glared at her.

"Leave Trace to me, and I'll never mention a single thing I read in the journal. Stay with him any longer and I'll break the news tomorrow on Christmas day. Two choices. Which one will it be?" Britney held up two fingers mockingly.

I was seething with an anger I'd never felt before, even when my mother had betrayed me. "He won't go back to you."

I knew Trace had seen behind Britney's weak façade.

"He will," she said adamantly.

"You're going to blackmail him, too? With what?"

"I can release Dane easily, or I can break his heart. Honestly, I don't care which way it goes. I can tell him he's a freak and I can't ever let him lay a hand on me again."

"Skank!" I spat out at her, wishing I had the ammunition to tell her to go fuck herself. Unfortunately, I didn't know what to do.

Every detail of our lives would be dissected, and I couldn't watch Trace go through that. The thing I didn't want was to see his father dragged through the mud after his death. It would kill all of the Walker sons. We'd known this was going to end. It was just going to have to be wrapped up sooner than we'd planned.

Britney eyes narrowed. "Decide," she demanded.

"I'll go. But know this...you'll never get Trace back. He already knows you're a whore, and he isn't going to be with you again. Ever."

"He loves his brothers. I was with him long enough to know his weaknesses."

Just the fact that he she'd use his love for his brothers against Trace made me nauseous. "Get. Out."

I didn't want her in Trace's bedroom ever again.

"I'll expect you gone by morning. And leave the ring." Britney looked at the vintage engagement ring. "He'll be giving that to me. I always wanted a Christmas engagement."

Over my dead body!

I wasn't going to keep anything that belonged to Trace, but *she* sure as hell would never wear it.

My fury finally reached the surface so it wouldn't be contained, and I walked over to Britney, lifted my hand, and bitch slapped her hard enough that her head turned to the side as I heard the satisfying crack of my hand connecting with her face.

"I said get out," I repeated between gritted teeth.

"You hit me, you lowlife piece of crap," she said furiously.

"Leave or I'll do it again," I threatened ominously, more than ready to break into a full-fledged cat fight. I was angry now, and I didn't know what to do with the burning rage. Britney might be a lot taller than I was, but she was skinny and I doubted she had much fight.

Her hand to her swollen cheek, she warned, "Be gone in the morning." Turning around, she flounced out the door.

Closing the door, I quickly locked it, knowing if I saw her again I might not be able to contain myself.

I flopped onto the bed, landing on my back. What in the hell was I going to do?

I have to leave.

All I really wanted was to talk to Trace, but I knew he'd tell me not to run away and he'd deal with the fallout. I couldn't let that happen. He'd looked so happy with his brothers around. I didn't want trouble because of my past, not when it affected Trace and his family.

The pain in my chest was excruciating as I thought of separating from him. Over the last several weeks, we'd grown closer and closer. I had no doubt that I was in love with him, and leaving him would leave a wound that would probably never heal.

I have to love him enough to let go.

And I did love him that much, and more. There had never been any real future for me and Trace. I needed to rip off the Band-Aid and deal with all of my pain so I could eventually move on.

I wouldn't have the promised job, but now that my record was clear, I could get something else.

I'll be okay. I'll be okay.

"Eva! The door is locked!" Trace's voice sounded from the other side of the door.

I jumped up, trying to stamp down my panic at the thought of being without him.

I flipped the lock on the door, let him enter, then closed and locked the entrance again.

"Are you okay?"

Wanting to break down in tears as I saw the tender compassion in his eyes as he looked at me, I hugged him, trying to memorize his scent.

His arms wrapped around my waist immediately and he just held me. "Hey, something is wrong."

"No." I denied it. "I just missed you."

"I think I'm glad," he said devilishly.

"Everything okay with your brothers?"

"It's good. I think Sebastian is moving to Denver to work with me."

He sounded relieved...and happy. My heart lightened slightly. I knew he wanted to be close to his brothers again, and it was happening. Little by little, pretty soon the broken Walker family would be put together again. "You sound happy."

"I am," he replied, sliding a hand down my back to squeeze my jean-clad butt. "There's only one more thing that I want this Christmas."

"What?"

"You," he answered huskily.

"You've already had me," I teased. God, I had to keep this conversation light.

He pulled back and I was mesmerized by the light in his molten green eyes. "I want you forever, Eva."

My heart skittered as I looked into his eyes. It was what I wanted, too, but it wasn't going to happen. But I wanted him to know something. "Look, I have to say something, and I don't want you to react, okay? I just have something I want you to know."

He nodded, but his expression was confused.

I took a deep breath. "Somewhere along the way in this fake engagement, it became so much more than just an act. I care about you, Trace. I don't know when, and I don't know how it happened. I just know it's true."

He opened his mouth to say something, but I covered his lips with my fingers as I continued. "You don't need to say anything. There are no expectations. I just wanted you to know, these have been the best weeks of my life."

"Don't act like you're saying goodbye, Eva," he said huskily, his eyes burning into mine.

He bent his head down and captured my lips before I could respond. His tongue penetrated my mouth with a determined purpose, and I opened to him. I needed him right now, had to be with him one last time.

"Fuck me," I demanded urgently the moment he released my mouth.

"I plan on it," he agreed, already stepping back to fumble with the zipper of my jeans.

CHAPTER SEVENTEEN

Eva

*W*e ripped and tore at each other's clothing like we were going to die if we didn't fuck in the next few seconds, and I can honestly say that was *exactly* how I felt. I was so hungry for Trace that I couldn't breathe, and my heart was racing like an out of control freight train.

I yanked at the heavy fisherman's sweater he was wearing as he knelt to shuck off my jeans and panties.

"Off," I panted, making him lift his arms to let me relieve him of the garment as I impatiently kicked out of the denims and lingerie he'd lowered to my ankles.

He stood and made short work of my sweater and bra while I fumbled eagerly with the zipper of his pants. My hands were trembling so badly that Trace finally took over and got rid of his jeans and boxer briefs himself.

I moaned as he pinned my hands over my head on the wall, his eyes wild and feral as he stared down at me.

"Fuck, Eva. What in the hell have you done to me?" he growled.

I couldn't answer. I just stared up at him as air sawed in and out of my lungs. Trace was raw right now, and he was breathtaking. My body was straining, vibrating with the need to have this man inside me.

"Please," I pleaded, wrapping my arms around his neck.

"Wrap your legs around my waist," he demanded as he released his hold on my hands.

I hopped up and he caught my ass with both hands, squeezing my butt cheeks as he shifted until he was perfectly positioned.

My breath hitched, my body greedy as I felt his massive cock slide inside my damp folds and along my clit. I started to drown in sensation as my pebbled nipples abraded along the hard muscles of his chest.

I could forget my own name when I was entwined with Trace like this; the feel and the masculine scent of him was enough to make me lose myself entirely.

"Hold on to me." His voice was commanding, but also raw and needy.

Like I was capable of doing *anything* else but hold him? He was the center of my universe right now.

I tightened my legs around his hips, urging him to fuck me.

Trace didn't disappoint me, his forward surge pinning me tightly to the wall as he thrust inside my sheath. "Oh, God. Yes," I screamed, wondering if I'd ever felt anything as good as his body connected to mine.

Spearing my hands into his hair, I leaned into his chest and kissed him, thrusting my tongue into his mouth as he began a punishing rhythm, pistoning in and out of my channel with a force that left me helplessly moaning against his lips.

His assault on my senses was merciless as I finally broke from the embrace to breathe, and his mouth started to devour every bare inch of skin he could reach. Trace's tongue trailed a path from my ear to my shoulders, then back up again.

"You're mine, Eva. You'll always belong to me," he said in a rough whisper.

Every nerve ending in my body fired as his low declaration vibrated against my ear. His fierce possessiveness made me burn even hotter, and I was desperate to climax. Every stroke of his cock rubbed his groin against my clit, and the brutal pace was driving me insane, and I could feel my orgasm starting.

His hand moved on my rear, allowing his finger to stroke along the crack of my ass and over the puckered opening of my anus. The sensation of the tip of his finger penetrating that forbidden opening fired a violent climax that seized my body like a small object being sucked into the path of a tornado.

"Trace," I screamed as he continued to pummel into me. My back arched and my head connected with the wall. I gripped his shoulders, my nails biting into the skin of his upper back.

"Fuck, yeah. Claim me, Eva. Mark the shit out of me because I sure as hell know I'm already yours." He groaned as he pinned me against the wall one last time, entering me hard so his cock buried itself to the root inside me.

I bucked in his arms in the throes of my climax, my short nails still embedded in his skin. Some animalistic urge that was roaring inside me *did* want to make him mine in any way I could, especially after he'd declared himself to me.

As my body started to relax, I let go of my vise-like hold on his shoulders and wrapped my arms around him with a sob that was part relief and part sorrow as he finished spilling his warm release deep inside my womb.

My body was satiated, but my heart was shattering. How could I leave this man, this wonderful male who now owned a part of my soul?

He carried me to the bed and gently laid me down after lifting the covers. I slid over and he lowered his body between the sheets. "What's wrong?" he asked as he tenderly folded me into his arms.

"Nothing," I lied, knowing he'd probably heard my brief, involuntary sound of sadness. "I think I was...overwhelmed." Well, *that* was the truth.

"I want to make you happy, Eva."

Trace made me ecstatic, which was why it was going to be so damn hard to pull myself away from him. "You do."

Neither one of us said a word and we laid with our bodies entangled, my head on his chest while I listened to the rapid, strong beat of his heart, wishing that there was *any* way I could stay with him. Unfortunately, I never found a solution, and I knew these moments were precious because they'd have to sustain me for a lifetime.

Several hours later, I was dressed again, watching Trace sleep with my back propped against the headboard.

I had packed a small bag with only things I desperately needed, like a few changes of clothes and some personal items.

I'd left his mother's ring next to his wallet and watch on the nightstand, somewhere I knew that he would find it almost immediately after he woke.

I wasn't sure how he'd explain my absence to Sebastian and Dane, but he'd think of something. The important part was that Trace's name wasn't dragged through the mud, nor was his father's.

Knowing Trace was a fairly sound sleeper, I let my hand lightly stroke his hair. "I have to go," I whispered to a sleeping Trace. "I don't want to, but I can't destroy your life by staying."

I sighed, knowing I had to get off the bed and force myself to go, but I was stealing every moment possible.

"I love you," I said in a low voice, tears streaming down my cheeks unchecked. "I'm sorry I never told you, but it would have been awkward and complicated, and I know you'd hate that."

In the distance, I could hear one of Trace's fancy clocks chiming the midnight hour, and I knew it was time to go.

"Merry Christmas, Trace," I murmured shakily as I palmed his cheek gently and then pulled my hand away.

I didn't look back as I rose and hefted the light tote bag onto my shoulder and snatched up the jacket I'd set beside it. My tears were flowing like a river, blurring my vision to the point that I could barely see the door as I reached it and fumbled for the handle.

I'd just turned the knob when a very strong, very large arm snaked around my waist and Trace's voice boomed loud enough to wake every soul in the house. "What in the hell do you think you're doing!"

"Trace, I have to go." I struggled, but my strength was no match for the furious male who had yanked my body against his.

"Bullshit. You aren't going anywhere. You fucking love me. I heard you say it," he rasped loudly.

I dropped the bag and the jacket I was holding as he lifted me up, strode over to the bed, and dropped me unceremoniously onto the sheets. I started to roll over and out of bed, but he quickly straddled my body and pinned my hands beside my head.

"Explain," he said in a clipped, angry voice.

I looked up at him, my cheeks still streaked with wetness from my tears. He was enraged, but I wasn't afraid of him. Even though his eyes were stormy and his nostrils flaring with anger, he wouldn't hurt me. "I can't explain."

"You damn well *can* explain, and you *will*."

I shook my head. "I can't."

"Tell me, Eva. If you have a good reason, I'll let you go."

My mind was racing with thoughts. "You promise?"

He nodded sharply one time.

Maybe telling him the truth was the only way he was going to let me leave. And I did have to go.

I took a deep breath and started to speak. "Britney knows everything. She stole my mother's diary. I think she read more of it than I have. If I don't go, she'll publicize everything, and she'll tell Dane that she only slept with him to get to you. She'll hurt him."

He looked confused. "That's it? That's a terrible reason. You aren't going anywhere."

"It's enough. She'll destroy your father's reputation, and yours. And she'll hurt Dane badly." I yanked at my confined wrists irritably and glared at him.

"Honestly, sweetheart...no, it isn't enough. I fucking love you, Eva. Do you think I give a damn what Britney does?"

He loves me? "You obviously heard me talking, so you know that I love you, too. I can't let her destroy you. She threatened to expose everything about your father getting duped into marrying my crazy mother."

"My father is dead, Eva. And I don't give a fuck what she says about me or you. But I doubt she'd even carry through on her threats. Dane already knows she's using him. She isn't going to break his heart."

"He knows? He isn't in love with her?" Admittedly, I'd never thought Dane acted smitten, but he was a quiet sort of man.

"No," he answered flatly. "Now let's talk about us."

I swallowed the lump in my throat as I looked up at him, speechless. His eyes were still burning with intensity, and I didn't see any signs that his anger was fading.

He continued when I didn't speak, "If you leave, you'll break me, Eva. I've never felt this way about any woman, but I don't think I can ever put the pieces of me back together again if you go. I need you to stay with me. Whatever happens, we'll deal with it together, but you can't run away. I can't handle that."

My heart squeezed until I felt like it was going to burst. "Why me?" I asked softly.

He loves me? I still wasn't able to wrap my head around that statement, and I didn't get why he'd want me. Oh, I knew he cared, but he loved me to the point where I was his weakness, a woman he desperately needed. *Me?*

"Why not you?" he asked in a calmer voice.

"I'm a mixed-race nobody, Trace. A woman who was in prison for most of her adult life—"

"Because your mother was a lunatic," he finished. "You're the strongest woman I've ever met. I think I knew from the moment you admitted that you didn't know Chloe that I was doomed. I just didn't want to admit it, so I convinced myself I just needed to fuck you. But it's not true. Hell, I do need *that*, but I need more than that. I need everything from you."

He sounded disgruntled, and I had to smile. "Do you think you can let me up?"

His grip on my wrists became gentler, and he finally pulled me into a sitting position as he grumbled, "I'll release you, but I won't let you go."

He got a firm grip around my waist and tugged me between his legs.

I sighed as I felt the warmth of his body against my back. "I want to stay with you, but I'm afraid of what Britney will do. I didn't want to go, Trace."

"You're not going, and I don't give a flying fuck what Britney does. She's out of here. I'll apologize to Dane for losing him his fuck buddy, but I need you more than he needs her."

I sat there for a moment, stunned. It had to be the first time in his life that Trace had thought about his own needs first, and I told him so.

"I have to this time," he admitted. "I wouldn't be worth a damn if you leave me."

I kicked off my shoes and let them fall to the floor, then I turned, positioning myself on my knees and wrapped my arms around his bare shoulders. "I love you. I thought my heart was going to break," I mumbled tearfully.

"I would have put it back together again, baby," Trace said huskily as he nuzzled my ear. "There's nothing I wouldn't do for you."

I clung to him as my tears fell again, landing on his bare skin as I hugged him to me. There was nothing I wouldn't do for him, either. I was convinced that he really didn't care if my past got out to the public. "It will get ugly if she talks," I warned, my fear still present even though I was completely convinced that he loved me. I really didn't want my past to cause him any pain in the future. It would kill me if he got hurt because of me.

"Don't care," Trace grunted. "The only thing that would hurt me is if you leave."

I crumbled as he spoke his candid response, and I was grateful to whatever fate had brought this amazing man into my life, the only person who'd ever completely believed in me.

I pulled back as his arm reached out to the bedside table and he snatched something from his nightstand. "You forgot this," he said in a slightly annoyed voice.

He had his mother's ring.

"I couldn't take *that*," I stammered, surprised that he would ever think I wouldn't have given it back.

He lifted my left hand and slid the beautiful ring back on my finger. "Take it now, then. I want you to marry me, Eva. Not pretend, but for real. Put me out of my misery and tell me that you'll be my wife, that you'll wear this forever."

I looked from my hand to his face, not sure if I was elated or terrified. Then, because I couldn't stop myself, I started to cry.

CHAPTER EIGHTEEN

Eva

The thought of having Trace in my life forever as my best friend, my lover, and my husband was overwhelming. *Things like this don't happen to women like me.*

I hugged him again, whimpering against his neck.

"Hell, is the thought of marrying me that depressing?" Trace asked, as he wrapped his arms around me tightly.

"No," I answered with a cough that sounded more like a sob. "It's amazing. But for a woman like me, it's pretty much a fantasy to have the man of my dreams ask me to marry him."

"I'm an asshole, Eva. But if you agree to put up with me, you'll make me the happiest asshole in the world."

I couldn't help it. I laughed. Trace might be arrogant, bossy and determined to have his way when he thought he was right, but his positive qualities outweighed those things by a ton. Besides, sometimes I actually liked his bossiness. When I didn't, we were bound to argue, but none of that mattered. We loved each other, so we'd always compromise somehow.

"You are a little bit bossy," I mused aloud.

"Agreed," he admitted readily.

"And I don't like it when you do what you think is right for me without asking me."

"I won't," he vowed.

My heart melted, and I couldn't tease him anymore. "But you're my Prince Charming, and you rescued me when I didn't want to keep trying anymore," I admitted tearfully. "You believed in me, and made me feel like a valuable person again. Pretty soon, I started to believe that I was, too. I have work to do if I'm going to find myself again and leave my past behind, but I know I want to do that with you. I'm not sure what I'm going to do with my life, but I know where I belong now."

"Where?" he asked nervously.

"With you," I breathed softly into his ear. "Always with you if you really want me."

"So is that a yes?" he asked huskily.

"Yes, please. I love you so much it hurts. I want to marry you." Fat tears were still rolling down my cheeks, but I didn't care. After what seemed like a lifetime of hell, I now had the most valuable thing I'd ever possessed in my life; I had Trace's love.

"I don't ever want you to hurt, Eva. I think we both need to put the past where it belongs: in the past. It's history. You were never guilty of anything but working your ass off to survive." His arms tightened possessively. "I'll give you everything in my power to make you happy. What were your plans before you were arrested?"

I sighed and laid my head on Trace's strong shoulder. "Culinary school. Isa was helping me get scholarships and finding me a school that allowed me to work while I was learning."

"In Colorado?"

I nodded.

"Thank fuck!" he exclaimed. "The last thing I want is to have to be away from you to make you happy. Do you still want to go to school?"

"More than anything," I said wistfully.

"We'll find the best school in the area, and you can feel free to try out new recipes on me," he said magnanimously.

I actually giggled because I was so happy. "Thank you. That's very nice of you."

"I'm a selfish bastard," he corrected. "You're an amazing cook."

God, I adored this man who made me feel like I could do anything. "I love you," I told him breathlessly, my heart hammering with the adrenaline of loving and being loved. "I'll cook you anything I'm capable of making. It's the only thing I can think of to give you something back."

"I don't care what you do, as long as you're happy. Cook. Don't cook." He flipped me onto my back gently and covered my upper body with his. His dark jade eyes were intense as our gazes locked and held. "Just love me and marry me."

The raw power that Trace always seemed to exude was still present, but the vulnerability that he was willing to let show in his eyes would have brought me to my knees if I had been standing.

I knew that it was time to let go, to release myself from my past. Everything that had happened was unfortunate, but karma had given me an unbelievable future, and a man who would never let me feel alone and afraid again. If I had to do it all again just to end up where I was now, I'd do it just to be with him. Maybe I'd still have an occasional nightmare, and I didn't know how I felt about my grandmother, but I could figure that out later. All that mattered was living in the present, and be grateful that fate had thrown Trace Walker into my path.

He was right. I was guilty of nothing except trying to be a better person. From now on, I needed to let go of my anger and hold my head up as high as I possibly could. I was young. I was incredibly happy. And I knew I was capable of doing good things. The Britneys in the world could go to hell.

I lifted my hand and cupped his jaw, letting my fingers play over his lips. "I love you, too, Trace. We'll let go of the past together."

"Deal," he agreed in husky voice. "I have something I want to give you, but I don't want to make you cry again."

He made it sound like me crying was worse than torture for him. Didn't he understand that I was actually tearful because I was overwhelmingly happy?

"I won't cry," I promised.

"Good." He grinned at me as he rolled out of bed and went to his closet and pulled out a framed picture from the bottom of his closet. "I didn't get a chance to wrap it and put it under the tree."

For a moment, I'd been temporarily highly distracted by his naked form, my eyes glued to the hottest, tightest ass I'd ever seen. Until he turned around, and I was greeted by the sight of his cock standing at attention. My eyes devoured every defined muscle as he moved back to the bed. God, would I always be rendered mute and stunned just by looking at him naked? Dressed or undressed, the sight of him always took my breath away.

I smiled back at him as I reached out to accept the large frame. It was at least a foot wide and similar in height, and it was heavy, probably because of the ornate frame. I turned it around, and I froze as I looked at the face that seemed to be looking back at me.

It was a picture of my father.

I gasped in surprise, and contrary to my promise, tears welled up in my eyes. "Oh, my God. How?"

I didn't have a picture of my father. I'd lost everything, including most of my personal items when I'd been incarcerated.

"I found it in public records, and I digitally restored and enhanced it. You look like him, Eva."

The original photo might have been a work ID, or a picture taken by a coworker. It was a close-up, head and shoulders only, but my dad was smiling into the camera, his broad shoulders covered by one of his usual navy work shirts.

My fingers were trembling as I traced the outline of my father's face inside the glass cover. "This is how I remember him. No matter how hard he worked, or how hard life was, he was always smiling."

Trace sat back down on the bed and put his arm around me. "Then you're very much alike," he observed.

We *were* alike. The prominent picture gave me back a little piece of my dad, and made me remember how proud I was to be his daughter. "How do I thank you for something like this?"

"Kiss me?" he suggested hopefully.

I took the picture and carefully set it on my bedside table. It was really too big to set on a shelf, but I'd figure out where to hang it later.

Wrapping my arms around his neck, I moved in closer and whispered against his lips, "Thank you." Then, I kissed him, pouring every emotion I was feeling into the embrace.

It was funny how our Christmas gifts were so similar. I'd actually bought a very large frame and inserted the pictures of him, his father and his brothers into the spaces provided, photos that seemed to be shoved in drawers all over his house. I thought it would look good in his office. Strange how both of us seemed to want the other to remember happier times, a time before our lives had ended up in ruin. That gift, along with a few other small items, was already wrapped and under the tree for him to open in the morning.

We both came out of the kiss almost breathless. Trace stood up and pulled me to my feet, slowly undressing me as though he'd been doing it for years before he lowered me gently to the bed, and tucked the sheets and comforter around me.

He went to the closet and quickly donned a bathrobe and moved toward the door.

"What are you doing?" I asked from my comfortable cocoon.

"Making sure Britney is gone by morning."

He left before I had a chance to say anything else, but he was back within in a few minutes.

Trace shucked the robe, turned off the light, and slid in beside me. "Done," he affirmed as he gathered me up in his arms.

I almost purred with contentment as our bodies met skin-to-skin. "That quickly?"

"Sweetheart, she's not as scary as you might think. She's a woman who preys on rich men. The last thing she'd do is spill secrets. It's not good for her future prospects."

"Is Dane okay?"

"Having her leave early was his idea. Once I told him she was threatening you, he was ready to get rid of her. He likes you. So does Sebastian."

"I'd like to tell them the truth eventually," I told him hesitantly. I'd always wanted a brother, and I planned on making Trace's family my own.

"Then tell them. You can decide whether or not you want to share your past. It doesn't matter to me in any way except that I hate how much you suffered."

I cuddled into his warm body, feeling so content that I couldn't move if the house was on fire. God, I loved the way he trusted my judgment, the way he was willing to accept anything I decided to do. "I'll think about it."

I was tired, and my eyes closed as I relaxed against him. "I love you so much. Merry Christmas, Trace."

"Merry Christmas, baby," he replied as he kissed me tenderly on the forehead.

As I drifted off to sleep, I marveled at the fact that this Christmas hadn't exactly gone the way I'd planned. I'd known that this job with Trace would change my life, but I just didn't know how much.

I never imagined when I'd went with plan 'A' the day I met Trace, that not only would I be saved from the streets, but I'd end up truly being loved.

For a woman like me who had never known a whole lot of love in her life, it was nothing less than a miracle, and the best gift I could ever receive.

I feel asleep with a smile on my lips and my arms wrapped tightly around my best Christmas present ever.

EPILOGUE

Trace

*A*ny *man who thinks getting married isn't stressful for the groom is a damn idiot!*

I was a nervous wreck as I waited in the ante room assigned to the groom and groomsmen, waiting for what seemed like forever to be called to take our places.

Dane looked uncomfortable in his black tuxedo that was very similar to mine, but he wasn't complaining. I knew it wasn't easy for him to leave his island to stand up for me at my wedding, and I was damn grateful he was there. I knew he was doing it for me... and for Eva. My youngest brother had become very fond of Eva, and since she called him several times a week, he was starting to become a little more social. My sweet Eva could be stubborn, and she had been pretty damned determined to see me, Sebastian and Dane become as close as we were when we were young.

Little by little...she was accomplishing her goal.

I'd kept the wedding small since Dane was acting as my best man. Sebastian was walking Eva down the aisle, a responsibility he was taking very seriously. In fact, my middle brother had become a model partner, which was giving me some extra time to spend with Eva before she started culinary school in the fall. We were departing for a very long honeymoon shortly after the wedding, a vacation where I hoped we'd spent a lot of time naked.

Even though I was nervous, I smiled just a little because I knew Eva. She'd be determined to see the sights in places she'd never been before. I'd be just as stubborn about wanting us naked and fucking until I could get rid of the constant erection I sported whenever I was near her.

We'd reach a compromise.

We always did.

"I'm off to go find the bride. It's almost time," Sebastian mentioned anxiously.

Hell, he sounded almost as nervous as I was. I looked at my middle brother, grateful for all the discussions we'd had about the past. We didn't talk much about it anymore, and I think we were past our differences. I hadn't known what he wanted, and he hadn't spoken up. We'd both taken our share of the blame and came out closer because of it.

"Don't scare my bride off," I grumbled as I looked at Sebastian who was dressed almost the same as me and Dane.

"I'm actually hoping she'll dump you at the alter and run away with me," Sebastian said mischievously.

I glared at him, but refused to let him goad me. There was nothing he enjoyed more than watching me get irritated and possessive. Honestly, I knew Eva was safe with Sebastian. He didn't poach in another man's territory, and he wasn't about to steal away with my bride. Besides, I knew that Eva loved me. Still, I didn't appreciate his humor right now.

"Just go find her and Isa, smart ass," I growled.

Sebastian just grinned and ambled off to find my bride and her Matron of Honor.

I'd gotten to like Isa and her husband, Robert. They'd both come over to the house for dinner several times now, and I found myself looking forward to those casual nights with company. Isa was a sweet woman, and her husband was a rich guy with a sense of humor. The two of them were always welcome, pleasant guests.

"Are you okay?" Dane asked curiously.

"Fine," I answered abruptly.

"You're looking a little nervous. I don't think I've ever seen you anxious before."

"I've never gotten married before," I replied drily. "I just want to get this over with. I just want Eva to be mine."

"Do you think she's going to run away? She's already yours, Trace. Relax."

Easy for him to say. He's never had a woman who had him by the balls. Not that Eva ever took advantage of that fact. But sometimes it was fucking terrifying to love someone that much.

"We're ready gentlemen," the wedding planner said from the doorway.

"Showtime," Dane said unhappily.

I followed the wedding planner, with Dane close behind me. We stepped into our places in the front of the church, and I finally looked out at the attendees.

Many of them were casual friends or distant relatives, but my gaze landed on an elegant woman in the front row, an older female. Nora Mitchell. She was sitting with her three stepchildren near the front of the church, and I knew Eva would be happy they were here. I couldn't say that everything was perfect in the relationship between Eva and her grandmother, but they were slowly working through the pain of the past. I was pretty sure that they had more happy times together than they did sad ones, and I knew that Eva had become fond of Nora's stepchildren.

My cousin, Gabe, and his wife, Chloe, were both grinning in the front row. I was wondering if my cousin wasn't enjoying my nervousness just a little since I'd teased him about how intense he was with Chloe before they'd gotten married. Now, unfortunately, I understood exactly how he'd felt. I glared at him unhappily before I shot Chloe a weak smile. Really, I was grateful to my cousin's wife, and the fact that her friend had gotten caught up in the holidays and hadn't showed up at my office to talk about being my fake fiancée. Indirectly, Chloe was responsible for me being with Eva now.

My heart started to speed up as the music fired up and Isa made her way gracefully down the aisle, shooting me an encouraging smile as she took her place across from me and Dane. As the guests stood for Eva, my gaze never left the door that I knew she'd enter from.

I held my breath as I saw her walking elegantly beside Sebastian, looking incredibly beautiful in the white wedding gown she'd chosen.

I didn't release my breath until Sebastian had brought her to me and she was safely at my side. I felt a strange, poignant ache in my gut when I saw that she was wearing the pearl necklace and earrings I'd given her. It had taken a while, but she'd finally learned how to accept the jewelry I bought her, taking one step further away from her fears of the past.

Strangely, my bride didn't look nervous at all, and her face was lit up in an enormous smile.

We turned forward, and I reached for her hand. "You don't look nervous," I said in a low voice that only she could hear.

"I'm not," she whispered. "This is my fairy tale. I'm going to enjoy it."

I grinned as I remembered that Eva considered herself some kind of Cinderella. And I continually reminded her that I was no Prince Charming.

I felt myself relax. I might not be some hero in a fairy tale, but as long as Eva kept looking at me like I was, it didn't really matter.

"I'll get my wish later," I said into her ear.

"Pervert," she said in a hushed voice, admonishing, but so full of teasing affection that I was no longer nervous.

Hell, I was marrying the woman that I loved more than anyone else in the world. Now that she was beside me, everything was all good.

"Are we ready?" the minister asked with a smile.

"Yes," we both said in perfect unison.

Eva and I turned our heads to smile at each other. Happiness was a heady feeling, but I was pretty sure I could get used to it. Neither one of us had experienced that emotion very much in the past. Maybe I'd had money and Eva hadn't, but we were profoundly connected in so many other ways that we understood each other's pain.

Now, we were learning to accept happiness as it was due, and we savored every minute of it.

Hell yes, I was ready.

"I think I've been waiting for this moment my entire life," Eva whispered as the minister opened his Bible and fumbled for the pages he wanted.

My heart soared at her words because I knew exactly what she meant. Every bit of pain and sorrow we'd experienced in our life had brought us to this moment.

I squeezed her hand to let her know I understood. "I'm waiting rather impatiently for the honeymoon."

A laugh escaped her mouth, totally destroying the solemn atmosphere, but for me, there was no better sound in the world. I smirked as she covered her mouth with her hand, trying to stifle her amusement at my irreverent comment.

She failed.

I caught her body as she threw herself at me and chortled with abandon, "I love you."

"I love you back, sweetheart," I whispered in her ear as I hugged her to my body, savoring her sweet smell.

The minister coughed, obviously a sign that he was now organized, but I ignored him until I was damn ready to let her go.

Finally, we broke apart, and I took her hand again, nodding at the gray-haired man to start the ceremony.

Maybe it *wasn't* how a fairy tale wedding should start, but this was us, me and Eva, and I thought laughter was a perfect way for our life together to begin.

The End

Please visit me at:

http://www.authorjsscott.com
http://www.facebook.com/authorjsscott

You can write to me at
jsscott_author@hotmail.com

You can also tweet
@AuthorJSScott

Please sign up for my Newsletter for updates,
new releases and exclusive excerpts.

Books by J. S. Scott:

The Billionaire's Obsession Series:

The Billionaire's Obsession

Heart Of The Billionaire

The Billionaire's Salvation

The Billionaire's Game

Billionaire Undone

Billionaire Unmasked

Billionaire Untamed

Billionaire Unbound

Billionaire Undaunted

Made in the USA
Monee, IL
24 October 2020